HER MAIL ORDER
MISUNDERSTANDING

LONDON JAMES

ONE

HARRISON

hose who have never met anyone stubborn haven't met Colt Reiner.

It was a thought Harrison Craig thought to himself more than once daily, and looking at the six-year-old, standing with his arms folded near a tree while his mama knelt in front of him, a thought he was sure his parents thought as well.

How could anyone not? Coming in contact with that child was like standing on the train tracks, holding their hand up, all the while thinking that they would have the power to stop a train chugging down the tracks at full speed.

Honestly, at times, Harrison thought the person trying to stop the train had better odds.

And from the look on Colt's mama's face, she might agree.

Watching the poor woman, Harrison had to chuckle to himself before he turned his attention back to the table of homemade pies, cakes, and an arrangement of cookies so loaded with sugar they made his teeth hurt just thinking about tasting them.

"Mr. Craig! Mr. Craig! Have you tried my pie?" Sadie

McCray came bounding toward her teacher. Her white-blonde curls bounced, and a smile spread across her face.

"I haven't yet, Sadie," Harrison answered. He paused for a moment, but then, taking in the sight of how fast her smile faded and disappointment flooded her face, he continued. "But I'd love to try some now. Do you think you could fetch me a slice?"

Her smile returned. "Of course, Mr. Craig. I'll be right back."

She darted off to one of the other tables filled with desserts. While it had been a wonderful idea to host a picnic for the children and parents at the start of the new school year, he hadn't thought to make sure families brought an array of dishes for everyone to eat. With little word on what to bring, everyone brought dessert, leaving an endless number of tables full of sugar, and only a few platters of meats, cheeses, and bread. Trays that emptied within minutes.

Up until then, it had been a secret that while Harrison was a master at teaching the children, his party planning skills lacked . . . severely.

"Good afternoon, Mr. Craig," a voice said behind him.

He turned to see Maggie and Cullen McCray approaching them and he nodded, shaking Mr. McCray's hand.

"Good afternoon to you both."

"I saw Sadie dart off in another direction. Did she say hello to you?" Mr. McCray asked.

"Yes, she did. She is getting me a piece of her pie."

"Ah, I see. Well, I have to say that you are in for a treat, and I'm not even being biased. She's turned into quite the little baker in the last few months."

"Then I shall look forward to the slice coming."

"We wanted to ask you how she is doing with her schooling," Mrs. McCray said. She cocked her head slightly as her husband wrapped his arm around her waist. Harrison followed the movement, trying not to watch, but failing.

While it had been a secret he wasn't much of a planner when it came to town functions; it was also a town secret about how much he longed for a wife of his own.

"She's doing excellent now that she's caught up."

"That's wonderful to hear. She talks non-stop about you and how much you have helped her."

"Well, she's a good girl, and she's learned quickly. I've had other children who weren't as far behind on their studies take months longer to catch up. You both should be proud."

"I am proud," Mr. McCray said, heaving a deep sigh. "Though I also am feeling guilty about letting her schooling slip as I did. Thankfully, this woman," he squeezed Mrs. McCray a little tighter, and the woman smiled, ducking her chin. "Put me in my place when it came to what the girl needed."

"I'm sure you would have figured it out if she hadn't. But there's always something to the orders of a woman that does wonders for us stubborn men." Harrison glanced over at Colt's mama, who was still kneeling in front of her son. A slight laugh snorted through his nose. "At least some of us men."

"Here you go, Mr. Craig," Sadie said, trotting back over to the three of them. The slice of pie bounced a little on the plate and tipped over as she halted in front of her teacher. Her cheeks turned pink, and she gave him a sheepish grin. "Sorry."

"It's quite all right. I'm sure it won't affect the taste at all. Besides, it all gets jumbled up in the mouth and stomach anyway, right?"

"Right."

He took the plate and fork from her, digging into his first bite while she watched. Her eyes were the size of the plate, and she bit her lip as though she waited on bated breath to see how much he liked it.

The sugar, cinnamon, and apples hit his tongue with a sweet, but tart jolt, and it blended perfectly with the flaky, buttery crust that all seemed to melt in his mouth.

"This is by far the best pie I've ever tasted, Sadie," he said.

A beaming smile spread across her face, and she grabbed the sides of her dress, holding them out to give him a curtsy. "Thank you."

She turned toward Mr. and Mrs. McCray. "I told you he would like it."

"And we never doubted you," Mr. McCray said. "Now find your friends and play. We will leave in about an hour to head home."

"But do we have to?" She stuck out her bottom lip in a pout.

"Yes, now, run along before I change my mind and we leave now."

Before Mr. McCray finished his sentence, she spun on her heel and darted off toward the play yard near the school where all the other children were playing. Her hair whipped from her haste, and she vanished before Harrison had a chance to even take another bite of pie.

"I have to say," he said to the McCray's. "This is the best pie I've ever eaten. She has amazing skills."

"Yes, she does. She's taken over most of the cooking in the house. Which I have to say has been a blessing at times when I haven't felt good." Mrs. McCray rubbed her hand over the small, growing bump of her stomach.

It was another move Harrison couldn't help but watch with a longing in his chest. He loved children—which was a given with his profession. Why would someone go into teaching if they didn't? But it was more than just loving how he helped shape the minds of the children he taught. He wanted children of his own. Boys, girls, it didn't matter. One, two, ten, the number didn't matter either. He just wanted a wife and a family. Period.

"Well, we won't keep any more of your time. We just wanted to extend our appreciation and see how she's doing."

The pair wandered off, leaving Harrison standing next to the table with a lonely little piece of half-eaten pie. There was nothing but families surrounding him. Mothers and fathers, husbands and wives, and although he often found himself as the odd man out, single and alone, there were only a few times the feeling had ever hit him this hard in the chest.

And today was one of those times.

"Mr. McCray?" He called after the pair, darting after them too as they both turned to face him. He glanced at Mrs. McCray, and his cheeks flushed with warmth. He couldn't ask with her listening. "Uh, might I have a word with you . . . alone?"

The two of them looked at each other and Mrs. McCray smiled, releasing her husband's arm. "Why don't I fetch myself a slice of that pie? Perhaps I can keep it down this time without retching it back up in an hour."

As she walked off, the two men watched her. Harrison's heart raced. He didn't know how Mr. McCray would take the question and he also didn't want to look like a fool.

"What is it you wish to speak to me about, Mr. Craig?"

"Well, I was wondering . . . if you don't mind my asking . . . where did you and Mrs. McCray meet?"

Mr. McCray blinked a few times, then he inhaled and exhaled a deep breath. "Well, it's funny you should ask. She came to Lone Hollow to marry Clint, my brother. She left her home before word could reach her about his death. I don't know how I could be blessed with such a miracle, but I thank God every day he gave me another chance."

"So, you didn't correspond with her before?"

"No. And I never asked her how she met Clint. I could if you wanted."

The warmth spread down Harrison's neck, and he shook his head. "Oh, no. No, that won't be necessary. I was just curious."

Mr. McCray studied him for a moment and the man's eyes narrowed. "You know, if you are looking for information on . . . women to correspond with, you might wish to speak to Mr.

Townsend. It was rumored that his father sent for Lily through a marriage broker or something like that. I'm sure he could get you in touch with whoever it was his father had contact with."

"Oh. All right. I suppose I will talk to him. Thank you."

Mr. McCray offered a smile and clapped his hand on Harrison's back. "Glad to have helped. Even if it was only a little." He moved forward a few steps, then turned to face Harrison again. "For the record, Mr. Craig. Having a wife and family . . . is more than I could have ever hoped for, and it's nothing to be embarrassed about if such is what you desire for yourself."

Harrison ducked his chin, giving a nod. "Thank you."

"Oh, and if you're looking for Mr. Townsend. He is over with Mayor Jackson. They are talking about plans to do . . . something. I'm not sure what. All I know is when those two get together, it usually ends up costing everyone in town money." Mr. McCray snorted a laugh, and with a slight wave, he strode off toward Mrs. McCray, who stood at the table, shoveling bites of pie into her mouth as though she hadn't seen food in days.

***

Just as Mr. McCray had said, Harrison found Mr. Townsend and Mayor Jackson over near the school. Lost in their conversation, both of their arms waved in the air excitedly, and as he caught their attention, they waved him over.

"Ah, Mr. Craig, we were just going to come to find you. We wanted to know what your opinion is about expanding the school," Mayor Jackson said.

"Expanding? But we haven't outgrown it. In fact, there is room for plenty more children before that happens."

"Well, yes, I am aware of that matter. However, Lone Hollow is growing, and I thought we should grab the bull by the horns so to speak, and be proactive on expanding the school when the town has a surplus of money to fund it, instead of after something happens and there is no budget to spend."

"But then what will happen if there is an emergency?"

"Oh, that's not something we should concern ourselves with. My focus right now is expanding the school so that Lone Hollow can continue to grow. More and more people are moving here, ya know. We might even need a second teacher one of these days."

"A second teacher?"

Mayor Jackson shrugged. "You never know." The plump man pointed his fat finger in Harrison's face and wiggled it. "And you would benefit from the help, too. Not that I think you're overworked. But having another teacher around can't be that bad."

"Yes, I know."

"Then it's settled."

"What is? Are you going to write for another teaching post?"

"Heavens, no. At least not yet anyway. No, I meant the plans to expand the schoolhouse. I shall start the plans first thing in the morning." He turned to Mr. Townsend, who had been overhearing the conversation, but who also had looked a little distracted with studying the dimensions of the schoolhouse. "And, Mr. Townsend, I will be in touch as soon as I know the amount of lumber we will need."

"I'll be waiting for the command to start, then."

"Yes, please do. Now, if you both will excuse me. I heard a charming little girl going on about her apple pie earlier and I must say, listening to her made my mouth water. I'm going to see if I can find myself a piece. If there is any left, I mean."

Harrison watched as Mayor Jackson meandered over to the tables, scouring them all until he found the pie tin he'd been looking for. A broad grin spread across the man's face, and he scooped up a slice, dumping it on a plate before grabbing a fork and digging in.

"Sometimes I don't know about that man's choices as Mayor," Mr. Townsend said, watching him, too.

Harrison snorted a laugh. "You and everyone else in this town. But somehow, we all voted for him, anyway."

"That's the odd part, is it not?" Mr. Townsend glanced at Harrison and the two laughed.

"Do you think it will be expensive to expand the school?" Harrison asked.

Mr. Townsend shook his head. "No. I'll make sure that it's not. It will be my contribution to the school considering you might be teaching my son or daughter when the time comes."

"So, Lily is . . ."

"Yes. We believe so."

"Congratulations."

"Thank you. We've been trying since the wedding last Fall, and while we didn't think it would happen so quickly, we are quite happy."

Harrison glanced over at the young man standing next to him, and while it wasn't a sense of jealously that plagued him, there was something there. Something he felt in his chest that almost made it hurt. Perhaps it was longing.

"Mr. Townsend, may I ask you something?" he asked.

"Of course."

"I was speaking to Mr. McCray, and he mentioned how you met Lily. Is it true?"

"That my father sent for her, and she was a mail-order bride?"

"Well, he didn't say those words exactly, but in a manner of speaking, yes."

Mr. Townsend nodded and gave a little smirk. "I'm not sure if I should be impressed with the gossip or embarrassed." He paused, chuckling again before he continued. "But to answer your question, yes, it is true. My father went through a marriage broker named Mr. Benson. I can get you the information if you would like."

"Oh, I don't know if I want to go through Mr. Benson just yet. I was just curious."

Mr. Townsend slapped Harrison on the back. "I'll tell you

what, why don't I write to Mr. Benson asking him if he has a young lady looking to correspond with a nice gentleman. If he does and writes back, then you can decide if you want to contact her. Sound all right?"

Harrison bit his lip for a moment. While the embarrassed part of him wanted to say no, the other part of him that longed for a wife and family screamed to say yes.

The latter won.

"All right. Thank you."

"It's not a problem. Now all I have to do is figure out how we are going to expand this schoolhouse."

TWO

AMELIA

*A*melia stumbled up to the schoolhouse door, dropping the books she had stacked in her arms. They hit the ground with a thud, and she groaned as she glanced up at the sky. "A little help, here," she said. "Just a little help."

The early morning air chilled through her jacket and the dew from the fog that rolled in overnight dampened not only her dress but the strands of her hair. She brushed her dark chocolate curls out of her face, ignoring how some hairs stuck to her cheeks as she bent down and fetched the books. The ones that landed on the bottom were covered in dirt.

"Just a little help," she said again. Her tone was more like a whisper on her annoyed breath.

After picking the books up and dusting off the dirty ones, she tucked them back under her arms and turned the doorknob, entering the schoolhouse and heading toward her desk without bothering to close the door.

It was the start of another school year and the start of what she hoped would be a better year.

With the books laid down on her desk, she moved around to the other side of the room, heading to the stove to not only light it but to add a bit of wood and kindling to reignite the fire. Her hot breath was visible in the cold room, and her fingers fumbled with the match, trembling as she lit it and then stuck it in the stove, watching as the flame burned the pine needles into nothing but black strings of charred bits and ignited the pinecones and chunks of wood.

She wanted to stand by the stove for the rest of the morning, but she knew she couldn't, and she moved over toward the blackboard, ignoring how the hairs on her arms stood in search of the warmth as she walked away from the stove. She grabbed a piece of chalk, writing a few sentences that she would have to teach that day.

Someone cleared their throat behind her, and she jumped, spinning to face the sound. She clutched her chest, letting out a sigh.

"Mayor Sheffield. You scared me."

"I'm sorry Miss Hawthorn. I didn't mean to. I should have announced myself at the door." The older gentleman ducked his chin as he removed the hat from his head.

"It's not a bother. What can I do for you, Mr. Sheffield?"

His brow furrowed, and he opened his mouth, only to close it before he said a word.

Her stomach twisted. "Don't tell me no students are coming to school today."

"I'm afraid there aren't. All but Billy and Suzy have moved away and now . . . well, Samuel's folks think he'd be better off doing his schooling at home so he can tend to more chores."

"More chores? Because this country functions on chores."

"Well, it kind of does. At least out here, it does."

"And so all children are just supposed to stay here in Brook Creek. A town that is losing residents daily. Pretty soon there won't be anyone living here at all."

"You think I don't know that? What can we do, though? The water is drying up and with other towns like Lone Hollow growing as they are . . . I can't keep people from wanting to live someplace where they can have a better life. Not to mention some of the newcomers who have moved here. Only men without wives or children, and some who don't look right. Like something's wrong with them."

Although Amelia wanted to disagree with the mayor, she knew she couldn't. She knew how the town was suffering to survive. So many families had already moved away, and the ones who remained . . . it was only a matter of time before they would be gone, too. She also knew of the men the mayor spoke of, and they had worried her too from time to time. Seedy types, only here to look for a drink in the saloon or a girl to warm their beds. It was getting so she didn't even wish to be out at night alone.

"So, that's it. What am I supposed to do?"

The mayor ducked his chin again, letting out another deep sigh as his shoulders hunched and he paced the floor of the schoolhouse. "I'm sorry to have to tell you this, Miss Hawthorn, but with no children . . . I have to close the schoolhouse."

Amelia sucked in a breath. She had a feeling this day was coming. The problem was; however, she had no other post— and no other job—to take.

What would she do now?

She couldn't return to the city. Not only had she no place to live, but she had no money to return home. She'd spent every last dime she had traveling to Brook Creek and hadn't had much pay since. It took all she had just to rent a small room from one of the families and keep food on her table.

"So, what is it you're saying, Mr. Sheffield? Are you saying I'm now out of a job?"

The old man paused and inhaled a breath. His belly stuck out several inches farther for a moment before he exhaled. "Well, I'm afraid so."

Tears misted her eyes, and she turned away from him,

nodding. It was the only thing she could think to do through her shock. Fighting back tears, she gathered the schoolbooks from the desks and stacked them on the bookshelf in the corner. A few of them had pencil marks on them from the few different children she had taught in the few months she'd lived in Brook Creek and while she never wanted to get too attached to them—it was always too hard if and when the time came, she would have to say goodbye—she couldn't deny, her heart broke a little with the sight of all the letters of their names.

"Because I knew this day was coming," Mayor Sheffield said. "I wrote to Mrs. Seymore about another post for you. She . . . she sent this, and it arrived this afternoon."

As Amelia turned and faced him, he stepped toward her, outstretching his hand to hand over an envelope.

"What is it?"

"I'm not sure."

She flipped it over in her hand and opened it, sliding the folded piece of parchment from the depths. She unfolded it, reading the letter from Mrs. Seymore.

My dearest Amelia,

What a mess I've made in sending you to such a small town. Please forgive me. Mayor Sheffield has made me aware of the situation, and after some digging, I have found some news that I think you might be happy to hear.

I know that when you were hired as a teacher; you inquired about a post in the town of Lone Hollow. While I don't have all the details as of yet, I have heard rumors of an advertisement of some sort coming in from the town and it was from the local teacher. There has been no formal request that I know of, however, I will make sure to let anyone know when it comes in, I have filled the post. If I were you, I would

relocate to Lone Hollow as soon as you receive this and wait for my
instructions to come.

I sincerely hope this letter finds you well outside of this predicament,
and I look forward to writing to you with all the details as soon as they
are given to me.

Sincerely,
Mrs. Jane Seymore

Amelia read the letter a second time and then a third. While she was still heartbroken over the town she'd just spent the last year in, she also couldn't help but feel a swell of excitement. She'd hoped and prayed for the post in Lone Hollow for a long time, and now it was hers.

It was finally hers.

"I am to leave for Lone Hollow," she said to Mayor Sheffield.

The old man smiled and nodded. "At least some good news came from this."

"Yes, it did. I am still sad for Brook Creek, though. Sad for the town, for the people. I loved the children I taught while I was here, and I hope I made them enjoy school."

"I'm sure you did." He gave her another nod, then motioned toward her desk. "I'll let you pack up. Take your time. I'll lock up the schoolhouse later this afternoon."

He watched her for a bit, then left the schoolhouse, leaving the scent of his aftershave as the only remnant that he'd been in the room with her.

Finally, alone, she gathered the crate she'd kept in the corner and began packing away her books. Each one rested on the one below it until they all were stacked inside. With those packed, she took to the rest of her belongings and stuffed them away in her bag before extinguishing the stove, grabbing the crate, and heading to the door of the school, shutting it behind her for the last time.

The little white building—once a place of hope and a sense of future—now felt hollow. Even if she had a new post to look forward to, there was a sense of loss and sadness. Like a disappointment that leaves a wound and never heals right.

I suppose that will be what Brook Creek will be, she thought to herself. A wound that will never heal right.

Her only hope now lay in another town and a teaching post she'd wanted for so long. It was finally hers, and in her excitement, as she walked away from her old schoolhouse, she couldn't even bring herself to glance over her shoulder. She didn't want to look at the past. Not anymore. No, all she wanted to do was look to the future.

The future in Lone Hollow.

THREE

AMELIA

*T*he town of Brook Creek hadn't ever screamed home to Amelia, and while she'd only been there a year, she always believed that when she arrived in the one place she thought she could call home forever, she would just know. Like she would step off the stagecoach and the sky would open up, casting rays of light down upon her as if God was telling her this was it. This was home.

Instead, Brook Creek had been the opposite.

Of course, the children were delightful, and the parents had been pleasant. But there was still no sense of home. There was no sense of anything except for the overwhelming feeling she was an outsider and always had been and always would be.

Lone Hollow, however . . .

Lone Hollow was that place, and from the moment she stepped off the stagecoach, she couldn't help but feel it.

"Here you are, Ma'am," the stagecoach driver said, handing her the two bags she had traveled with.

"Oh, thank you."

"Not a problem." He tipped his hat and continued helping

the other passengers with their luggage while Amelia crossed over the porch and stepped through the hotel doors.

She'd been here once before. Well, been through the town, passing through on her way to Brook Creek. Although she had prayed every night that she would one day return, she was still in shock that day had come.

"Good afternoon." A man greeted her from behind a desk. "Are you looking for a room?"

"Yes, I am."

"And is it just for you?" He moved a little to the left, grabbing a ledger from the corner of the desk. He flipped it open and picked up the pencil that lay inside.

"Yes, it's just me. The name is Amelia Hawthorn."

"All right. And how long are ya wanting the room for?"

Amelia opened her mouth but then shut it. She didn't know when the teacher was leaving or if he or she had already left, and not knowing that she also did not know about the housing. "Um, I'm not sure exactly. I'm waiting for my post orders."

"Post orders?"

"Yes, for the teaching post."

The desk clerk jerked his head slightly, lifting one eyebrow. "Oh, I didn't know we were getting another teacher."

"Well, I don't know if it's been announced yet." Her heart thumped. "You know, if you could just forget I said anything and just put me down for a week's stay, that would be fine."

"All right. That will be two dollars a night. You can pay per night just in case you don't need the room that long."

"Oh, all right. That sounds like a fair deal." She reached into her bag, ignoring the fact that she didn't have the money for a week's stay. Hopefully, she wouldn't need it as hopefully, she would get her housing within just a day or two. "Here it is."

The man hesitated for a moment, then jotted down her name and took the money she held out for him. With the last of his pencil stroke, he closed the book. "Let me just get you the key and I'll show you to the room myself. Do you just have the two bags?"

"Yes, just the two."

"All right. I'll get them for you."

He handed her the room key before moving around the desk and grabbing her bags. A slight humph sound left his lips and by the time they reached the top of the stairs to the second floor of the building, a thin layer of sweat glistened on his forehead, down the sides of his face, and along the back of his neck.

"I can get them into the room," she said, not wanting the man to further exhaust himself.

"Oh, all right. Well, enjoy your stay. Let me know if there is anything I can get you."

"Is there a café in town?"

"Yes, ma'am. Just down the street. Boots Café. It's owned by Jeremiah 'Boots' McGee."

"McGee. Is he from Ireland?"

"Yes, ma'am."

"Well, thank you."

"You're welcome."

She watched as the man trudged back down the stairs, wiping his face with a handkerchief nearly the whole way back down to his desk.

~

*A*fter getting her things unpacked and settled, Amelia went back down the stairs and back out into the streets of Lone Hollow. Men and women traveled by foot and wagon in all directions, and they all either smiled or offered her some sort of greeting as they passed her.

Such a friendly place, she thought to herself. *And to think I am a stranger.*

Of course, she would only be a stranger for a short time, as she was sure once the mayor knew of her arrival it would be announced then everyone in town would know who she was.

And thinking of the mayor, she made a mental note to find him as soon as she was finished with supper. The quicker she got the housing situation to her liking, the sooner she could move from the hotel and not have to pay for the room.

Just as the desk clerk had said, she found the café down the street. The scents of home-cooked meals wafted around the building even outside and as she entered, her mouth watered, and her stomach growled.

Noticing how busy the place was, she scoured the nearby tables for a seat. None could be found, though, and she bit her lip at the thought of having to either wait a long time for a table to open up or come back at a later time.

"Excuse me, but my husband and I were just leaving," a woman said, approaching her. Amelia turned toward her, stopping herself before she could utter a word of thanks.

"You," she said, recognizing the woman.

The woman's head jerked, and she cocked it to the side. "I beg your pardon."

"I know you. Or at least I've met you before. I cannot think of where though."

The woman stared at her for a moment, then her mouth gaped open, and then she smiled. "You were on the stagecoach when I was traveling out to Lone Hollow. Amelia, isn't it?"

"Yes, it is. And you are . . . Maggie."

"Yes. Maggie McCray."

"You were traveling to Lone Hollow to marry a man with a daughter."

"Yes, I was."

Amelia noticed the woman's growing stomach and pointed toward it. "I see you married your man, and now are expecting. How lovely."

"Well, I married, but not the man I came here for. Unfortunately, when I arrived, I found out the man I came here for had died."

"Oh, goodness." Amelia clutched her throat. "I'm so sorry for your loss."

"Thank you. But I still have my happily ever after. I married his brother, and we are raising Sadie, his niece, as well as preparing for a little one of our own."

"Well, I'm glad you found him and I'm happy that Sadie has you in her life."

"Thank you." Maggie paused. "So, what are you doing in Lone Hollow? Weren't you at a teaching post in . . . oh, what was the name? I remember it was two synonyms for . . . river, wasn't it?"

Amelia nodded. "Brook Creek."

"Yes, Brook Creek. Weren't you at a teaching post there?"

"Yes, I was. But the town isn't surviving as well as everyone thought it would. More people have left, and they took their children with them. Without any students, I found myself without a post. It was then I was told of the post here, in Lone Hollow. And of course, I jumped on it."

Maggie's brow furrowed, and her head jerked again. "A post here? For a teacher? In Long Hollow?"

"Yes."

"Are you sure?"

"I'm quite sure. I was told that an advertisement had been made and since I expressed an interest in the town a long time ago, they contacted me."

"That's so odd. I didn't think Mr. Craig was leaving."

"Who is Mr. Craig?"

"Harrison Craig. He's the teacher here in Lone Hollow. I didn't know he was leaving."

"Well, perhaps he just didn't want to tell anyone until a replacement was found."

Maggie hesitated at Amelia's words, but then gave a half-smile and nodded. "Perhaps. Well, my husband and I best be on our way. You're more than welcome to our table."

Before Amelia could say much else than bid them both a farewell, they left the café, letting the door shut with an oddly loud thump, making Amelia wonder if it was something she said.

Surely, it wasn't, she thought. Nevertheless, she couldn't help but wonder.

Shoving the thoughts from her mind, she sat down at the table, scooting the chair in as a plump, red-headed man approached her.

"Good evenin'," he said, nodding to her as though he was tipping a hat to her, even though he wasn't wearing one. "What can I get yeh?" His thick Irish accent purred.

"You must be Mr. McGee."

He smiled, giving her a wink. "Don't know about the mister part. Everyone here just calls me Boots."

"Well, Boots, do you have a menu?"

His eyebrows furrowed for a moment, then he scratched his head. "Don't say that I do, ma'am. People around here just seem to know what they want."

"All right. What is it they order?"

"I got stew, and it's good and filling for a crisp fall night like tonight should be."

"Then I'll have that."

"Comin' right up. I'll bring yeh some cornbread too. Yeh, like butter?"

"Yes, I do."

"Cornbread and butter it is. I'll be back in a bit."

Before she could say a word of thanks, he trotted off, leaving her to finally glance around at the other patrons dining at the café. It was an odd mixture of a lot. A few men, several women, and one couple with a gaggle of children who all sat at the table, shoveling bites of food into their little mouths. Some conversations were loud. Some were quiet, and while a few people would glance in her direction, the rest simply ignored her.

It wasn't long before Boots returned, setting down a bowl of stew, a plate of cornbread and butter, and a glass of water in front of her.

"Here yeh are, ma'am. My famous beef stew."

"Famous, huh? Well, I can't wait to dig into it."

"Well, I hope yeh like it." He gave her another nod then darted off, back through the door he had vanished in once before.

She guessed it was the kitchen and shrugged off the wonder as she picked up a spoon and dug into the meal. The hearty, rich flavors warmed her belly and after several bites of stew, she grabbed a chunk of cornbread and slathered on several pats of butter.

"Excuse me?" a male voice said above her.

She glanced up, halfway through, taking a bite of cornbread, and froze.

The man smiled. "I was wondering if I might take that seat." He pointed toward the open chair not across from her, but diagonally at her table.

She gaped at him, and with her mouth full of cornbread, she couldn't answer.

"It's just that there are no other tables open." He pointed around the room, and her gaze followed his finger. It was true. There were no open tables or chairs in the room.

She chewed her bite, swallowing it a little too soon and the lump of food caught in her throat for a moment.

"I suppose that's all right," she said, still struggling to get the bite down. It finally went down, and she sipped at her water. Her eyes watered from the slight pain as it dislodged and went down.

"Thank you. And don't worry." He held up a rolled-up newspaper. "I won't be a bother. I'm just going to get my stew and read my paper."

She wanted to say something but didn't know what, so she nodded and turned her attention toward her meal while he sat down and opened the paper, hiding from her view. The sudden presence of someone else at the table set her on edge. She didn't want to appear rude, but it was odd. It was just odd.

~

HARRISON

*H*arrison hid behind his paper, keeping it above his face so he wouldn't have to look at the woman sitting across the table. He hadn't wanted to ask her to share, but he was hungry, and he had a lot of stuff to do that night. Supper couldn't wait.

Although she seemed friendly enough, he also didn't wish to make the situation even more awkward by adding in conversation.

"Why, Mr. Craig, I wasn't expecting you for another hour," Boots said, walking up to the table. He glanced between Harrison and the lady. "Oh, sorry for the interruption."

"There's no need for apologies, Boots," Harrison said, flipping down the newspaper so he could not only talk with the café owner but see the woman. "This kind lady allowed me a seat at her table since no others were available."

"Oh." Boots looked between the two of them once more. "Well, what can I get yeh?"

"Just some stew. I've got a long night ahead of me, so make it a double. And some of that cornbread with lots of butter."

"Of course, Mr. Craig. I'll be back in a bit." Boots meandered back to the kitchen, stopping by a few tables to not only see to the customers but refill their water glasses.

Harrison watched him for a second, then turning his attention back to the newspaper, he caught sight of the woman staring at him out of the corner of his eye. His heart thumped, and he inhaled a breath, finally looking at her.

"May I help you with something?" he asked.

She blinked at him. "You are Mr. Harrison Craig, the teacher?"

"Yes, I am."

"Then you are why I'm here."

Harrison's heart thumped again. Only this time it was harder, and it continued to race, beating faster and faster while heat trickled up the back of his neck. He had known this day was coming after receiving a letter from Mr. Benson, the marriage broker that he'd made a match. The only problem was he thought they would be corresponding by mail first.

"I'm sorry, I'm afraid I wasn't given your name."

"It's Miss Amelia Hawthorn."

"Well, it's a pretty name."

"Thank you."

"So, I have to say that I thought we would be corresponding by letter first." He straightened his shoulders, pressing his back into the back of the chair as he cleared his throat.

This night just got a lot more awkward, he thought.

"Oh. I wasn't told that. I was told to get on the first stagecoach to Lone Hollow, so that is what I did. Mrs. Seymore said that details would follow, so I'm waiting to hear from her."

"Mrs. Seymore?"

"Yes, isn't that who you spoke with?"

"No. I spoke with Mr. Benson."

"Huh. I don't know him. No matter though. I'm sure one of them will send me the details."

Although he was confused over what details this woman needed, he didn't ask. Instead, he nodded and leaned forward, resting his elbows on the table.

"Well, I suppose we should have dinner. A proper dinner. Does tomorrow night sound good?"

"Yes, it does."

"All right then."

"And I should probably come by the house and the school, too. Just to check on things, make sure it's all in order, you know."

His breath quickened and even more heat inched up the back of his neck. There was no hesitation about her. She just was jumping into the water, feet first, and with no look of concern or worry about her. He was almost envious of it, and yet, he was also a little scared of it.

"Oh. All right." He nearly stuttered over his response, and he watched as she continued to scoop her meal into her mouth. A sense of haste spurred through her movement, and she only looked him in the eye a few times.

By the time Boots brought out his supper, she had finished, and she stood and followed him up to the cash register, paying for her meal, and giving Harrison a wave before leaving.

"What on earth just happened?" he whispered to himself.

FOUR

AMELIA

*A*melia dressed the next morning, trying to ignore how each time she thought of what happened last night at the café caused her pulse to race. It hadn't been one of her finer moments. Shoveling down the stew—and burning her mouth—like some sort of wild beast who hadn't had a meal in weeks. Not to mention her boldness, inviting herself to Mr. Harrison's house and the schoolhouse without even a pause to think if it was proper. She'd been so flustered, even if she'd tried to hide it.

Not only from the shock of coming face to face with the teacher she was replacing, but for how attractive he'd been. And while she didn't want to admit it, there was a little sadness at the thought that he was leaving. Of course, her priorities had always lied in teaching and the children, but she couldn't deny that she thought of finding a husband and having children of her own.

Don't all women want those things? She thought.

She certainly was no different from them.

"Oh, stop it, Amelia," she said, buttoning the last button on her sleeve around her wrist. "You have one thing to focus on right now and that is getting the school set up, and the children transitioned over to a new teacher. Not to mention, you need to introduce yourself to the parents and show them you desire only the best for their children."

With her pep talk, she moved over to the mirror, glancing at her reflection in the glass. Although she needed a new wardrobe, it was something that would just have to wait. A lack of funds aside, she didn't have the time for it now.

Perhaps in a few weeks, when everyone was settled, and she had received some pay.

Something for her to think about.

~

*T*he walk across town had done little to comfort her feet. She hadn't thought a town such as Lone Hollow would have their schoolhouse so far from town but given that everything else about the town had been a mystery to her, she supposed she shouldn't have been surprised.

By the time she reached the steps of the front door, she'd probably walked a mile, at least.

No matter. She would think of it no more today. Today was for meeting the children. Today was for making a good impression, and with those thoughts on her mind, she inhaled a deep breath, straightened her shoulders, and entered the schoolhouse, shutting the door behind her.

"Good morning, children," she said.

Every child in the room spun in their seats. Their eyes widened in shock and a few of them had mouths gaped open. Mr. Craig sat at the desk in the front of the room—equally surprised and as he stood, she made her way toward him.

"And good morning, Mr. Craig."

His eyebrows furrowed but then, upon his noticing the children, they softened, and he nodded toward her. "Good morning, Miss Hawthorn."

"I wanted to apologize for my tardiness this morning. I didn't realize the schoolhouse was so far from town."

"Well, we have a lot of farms around here and some children travel quite far to attend school."

"Yes, I can see how that would warrant the distance, then. I will make sure to make a note of it from now on, however, and I shall never make the mistake of being late again."

Mr. Craig's eyebrows furrowed again. "Late again? I don't understand."

"Well, it's not proper for a teacher to arrive late to her class."

He blinked and leaned toward her, folding his arms across his chest. "I'm sorry, but a what?"

"A teacher should never be late to their class."

He opened his mouth, but then shut it, staring at her for a good long minute before trying—and succeeding—to speak again. "While I have to agree with you, Miss Hawthorn, I'm trying to understand why you think you are supposed to be here when I'm the teacher of this classroom."

"Well, yes, I know. You are the teacher. That is until you leave. When is that, by the way? I still haven't received the details of this post."

He gaped at her once more and shook his head as though he was not only stunned into silence but stunned in disbelief. Her heart thumped. Had she done something wrong? Had Mrs. Seymore been meaning to fire him and hadn't told him yet?

"I . . . I don't know what to say."

"Honestly, Mr. Craig, I'm failing to think of what to say myself. Did you or did you not place an advertisement for a replacement because you are leaving this post?"

All the children in the classroom gasped and one girl with white-blonde hair burst into tears. "You aren't leaving us, are you Mr. Craig?" she cried out.

Another boy, the oldest in the room, stood. His body

towered over everyone, and he clenched his fists and jaw as though he'd just heard the worst news of his life.

Mr. Craig moved over to the girl's desk, holding his hands out and laying them on her shoulder. "No, I'm not, Sadie. Don't you worry." He glanced up at all the children. "Don't worry, children. There seems to have been a mistake made. However, I assure you I'm not leaving Lone Hollow or my post as your teacher. And Hal," he said to the older boy. "You can sit down. Everything is all right."

Amelia's gut twisted with his words. What had happened? What had gone wrong? Surely, there was an obvious reason for all this mess.

"So, you did not place an advertisement?" she asked him, not fully wanting the answer, for she feared what it was, and yet, needing it all at the same time.

"Well, I placed an advertisement with Mr. Benson." The children gasped again, and he held out his hand as though to reassure them. "But it wasn't for a teacher," he said, raising his voice for all of them to hear.

"Well, then what was it for?" She rested her hands on her hips. A slight flicker of anger sparked in her chest. Now, what was she supposed to do? This was a mistake to end all mistakes, and she had the sudden realization that she was not only out of a job again, but also losing the town she'd dreamed about her whole life.

He glanced at the children once more, biting his lip.

"Well?" She pressed again. Her annoyance blazing more and more like flames that suddenly hit an open forest plagued with drought and dry as a bone.

"May we please take this conversation outside?"

"No, I would like an answer."

"And I will give it to you outside."

"Why?" She narrowed her eyes. "Why don't you want to say

anything in front of the children? Is it bad? Would their parents not approve?"

"I just think this is a conversation that should be between us."

"Well, I'm not leaving." She folded her arms across her chest and stomped her foot. "So, you can just tell me right here, right now."

He inhaled and exhaled a deep breath. His jaw clenched and his left eye twitched. He leaned in toward her, lowering his voice. "I placed an advertisement for a wife." A few of the boys and girls sitting near them laughed, and he shot them all a look that quieted them immediately. "It's something a lot of men do," he said to them. "Mr. and Mrs. Townsend—" He paused and closed his eyes as he let out a groan. "Of course."

"Of course, what?"

"Of course, he would do this."

"He? He who? Would do what?" Her annoyance was boiling now. She wanted to scream at him for not making sense.

"Mayor Jackson. He was going on and on about expanding the schoolhouse and hiring a second teacher. The town hasn't voted for the extra cost, however. He swore he was only just thinking of the idea. I didn't think he'd make the plans with no one agreeing to it." Mr. Craig ran his hands through his hair. "We need to go see the mayor. Let him sort out this mess because it was more than likely him who placed the ad for another teacher."

"All right, let's go see this Mayor Jackson. I have to say it's good to know this wasn't the mistake I thought because I can assure you, Mr. Craig, I did not come to Lone Hollow to be your wife."

FIVE

HARRISON

*H*arrison scaled the steps to the mayor's office. The handwritten note from the mayor rested in the palm of his hand and he squeezed the piece of parchment, causing it to wrinkle. He heaved a sign, entering through the door and shutting it behind him. He didn't want to be here anymore than he wanted to go see the doctor about any ailment. He hated doctors. And he hated meetings with the mayor. Especially when it was because of his job.

Miss Hawthorn sat in a chair outside the mayor's office door, and she glanced up at him as he made his way over to her and sat in the chair next to her. Although pretty, he couldn't help but feel slightly annoyed at her. She was the reason for this mess. She was the reason he was here.

"You got a note too?" she asked.

He didn't answer, but instead held up the paper and nodded, keeping his gaze focused on the door across the room. He didn't even want to look at her.

"Well, at least we will hopefully figure out what happened," she said.

They both waited in silence and Harrison looked up at the

clock on the wall, watching the second hand tick around the face. Minute after minute ticked by, and all he could think about was how he had so many other things he could have been doing with his time.

"Does he know we are here?" he finally asked Miss Hawthorn, not wishing to speak to her, but he needed to ask someone the question.

She nodded. "He knows I'm here. I don't know if he knows you are."

Harrison groaned as he leaned forward and vacated the chair. He made his way over to the door, knocking on it. "Mayor Jackson?"

"Yes?" the mayor said from the other side. "Who is it?"

"It's Mr. Craig and Miss Hawthorn, Mayor Jackson. We are both here and got your notes to meet."

"Oh, yes, yes. Come in."

Harrison held the door open and waited until Miss Hawthorn passed through it to enter the mayor's office. He didn't want to think about the sweet scent of her perfume and how it tickled his nose.

"Ah. Sorry to keep you waiting. I knew Miss Hawthorn was here, but I thought we were waiting for you, Mr. Craig."

"It's no trouble, Mayor Jackson," Miss Hawthorn said.

The mayor motioned for them both to take a seat in front of his desk, and as they both sat, he grabbed a few papers off the corner of his desk.

"I'm sorry for the delay in getting back to you, Miss Hawthorn, but I had to write to Mrs. Seymore to clarify why she sent you here."

"So, you didn't ask her to send her?" Harrison asked.

"No, I didn't." The mayor removed his spectacles and folded the earpieces before setting them down on his desk in front of him.

"So, what happened, then?"

"We don't know. The best we can figure is . . . well, we don't know what to figure. However, it seems that a Mrs. Benson, who is Mrs. Seymore's secretary, might have something to do with it. Her husband is a—"

"A marriage broker," Harrison finished. He leaned back in his chair, letting out a deep sigh as he closed his eyes for a moment. It was nothing more than a misunderstanding between advertisements.

A horrible misunderstanding.

And one that had caused a gigantic mess.

"Yes, that was what she said." Mayor Jackson glanced between the two. "It could have been that the papers were mixed up somehow. Although, I don't know how it could have happened." He shrugged.

"I thought you had placed the advertisement because of the expansion," Harrison said.

"Oh, no. I didn't do that. I'm not sure the expansion will happen. It still has to be voted on and even with a discount on the wood . . . I'm afraid it might cost more than people want to pay right now. I was going to bring it up at the next town meeting."

Harrison glanced over toward Miss Hawthorn. She sat with her chin tucked down toward her chest. Her gaze fluttered from side to side, and she blinked several times. He didn't want to doubt her ability to teach a classroom, but he'd seen what some of the older boys could pull and her behavior now . . . it left him questioning not only her qualifications but her training.

"Well, if they vote on it, Mayor, I would like to be not only notified, but help in the search for another teacher as I know what to look for and how to tell if someone is qualified."

Her head whipped toward him, and for the first time that afternoon, her gaze held his for a lot longer than just a few seconds.

"Excuse me, Mr. Craig," she said. "But are you trying to imply that I'm not qualified as a teacher?"

"No. At least not fully. I'm not sure of your qualifications.

"Well, then perhaps you should ask before just assuming. Because I would bet you I'm not only more qualified than you think, but perhaps even more qualified than you."

"Oh, you think so?" He slid around, facing her in his chair.

She mimicked his movement. "Yes, I do."

"And I bet you think you could teach my students better than I could, don't you?"

"As a matter of fact, I do."

"And you probably think you could make the parents love you so much they would beg for you to replace me as their children's teacher."

She hesitated for a moment, then straightened herself in the chair, squaring her shoulders. She lifted her head, stiffening her neck. "As a matter of fact, that is exactly what I think."

"Then prove it."

Her mouth gaped, and her shoulders hunched slightly. "I beg your pardon?"

"Prove it. You take over my schoolhouse for . . . two weeks. If at the end of the two weeks you have won over the children and the parents, then you can have my post as teacher in Lone Hollow."

While a part of him wasn't sure what he was saying, and screaming for him to shut up, he didn't listen. Instead, he listened to the other part of him, egging him on to make this bet —a bet he was sure she wouldn't be able to win. He knew his students, and he knew the parents. They weren't open to change, and they would see her—a newcomer—as a change they wouldn't like. Period.

"Are you seriously betting me for your position?" she asked, blinking at him.

"Yes, I am."

"Wait one minute." Mayor Jackson held up his hand. "Don't I have a say in this? It is my town. Or the parents?"

"But the parents will have a say. If at the end of two weeks, they prefer Miss Hawthorn, then they will get that chance to vote." Harrison glanced from the mayor to Miss Hawthorn, then back to the mayor. "Believe me, I doubt she will win."

"I'm sitting right here."

"What is your point?"

"My point is it's rude to talk about a person like they are not in the room when it's clear that they are."

"I'm still confused about your point. I'm not being rude. I'm being truthful. If you think the truth is rude . . . well, then Miss, you have bigger problems than trying to convince my students and my town that you are better than me."

"Oh, I highly doubt I will have any problem in that area. I can be quite charming and if this is how you are," she wiggled her finger at him. "Then I shouldn't have a problem."

"You were much nicer the first time we met."

"You mean when you thought I was here to be your wife?"

The mayor snorted a laugh, and Harrison turned toward him, pointing in the man's face. "It's a perfectly acceptable way to find a wife."

The mayor held up his hands. "I believe you."

"It's funny you should mention me being nicer when you first met me because I could say the same for you. Now that I see the truth . . ." She stared at him for a moment, then turned to the mayor. "I do have one minor issue, however, with all of this."

"And what is that, Miss Hawthorn?"

"Well, as you can imagine, it cost me a lot to uproot my home and move to Lone Hollow. Plus, I thought I would be provided with housing here, and since I'm currently staying in the hotel, you can bet it's a great expense . . ." She let her voice trail off, hoping the mayor would understand what she was trying to say without making her say the words.

"Do you want the town to cover the cost of your room and board, Miss Hawthorn?" the mayor finally asked.

She sat a little straighter in her chair and hesitated for a moment, as though she was debating on how to answer the question. It was the first little sign of weakness to her that Harrison saw, and it made him uncomfortable. As though he was causing her suffering. And him feeling angry with the woman or not, he didn't want to cause her strife.

"I will cover the cost of the hotel room," he said.

"I do not need your charity, Mr. Harrison," she said.

"Well, obviously you do."

"Fine." Her voice cut through the air. "However, please know that I will pay you back upon winning this bet and proving I am the better teacher for the children of Lone Hollow."

"And what will you do if you lose?"

She shot him a glare, opening her mouth, then closing it without saying a word. For a moment, he wished she would have just said what was obviously on his mind. He would have liked to have had a bit of amusement at the comeback she thought of attempting. He didn't wish to be rude, and he certainly didn't go into this meeting with even the tiniest spark of anger. But sitting here alone was enough to get annoyed with. Then she had to say she was a better teacher.

Nope.

He wasn't having it.

And he would, at the end of two weeks, prove how wrong she was.

SIX

AMELIA

*A*melia's heart thumped as she made her way back to the school a few days later. It was the first day she would have with the children, and while this was hardly the first time she'd introduced herself to a new classroom full of children, there was a difference about this time. This time was more significant. This time, she not only had to make sure the children were educated, but they had to like her.

No, no. They had to love her.

She never wanted to be a reason someone lost their job. Especially another teacher. However, not only did she want the teaching position in Lone Hollow, she wanted to take it from Mr. Craig.

She thought of how he had behaved in the mayor's office and how rude his arrogance had been. She didn't want to think he could be the type of man to act that way; however, she supposed she'd been wrong about him. For that was how he acted.

The walk to the schoolhouse had been just as long this morning, and yet, had passed in no time as she soon found herself—not only on time—but at the front door, and she hesitated before opening it up. The basket hooked on her arm trembled slightly, along with the rest of her body. Tucked inside was not only her lunch but a few books she thought would help her today.

"You're going to do fine, Amelia," she whispered to herself. "You'll be just fine. No child has ever not liked you and you know what you are doing."

With an inhaled breath, she opened the door.

Mr. Craig stood at the head of the class and as she stepped inside the schoolhouse, all the children spun in their seats facing her. Their wide eyes blinked, and they watched her walk through the schoolhouse and up to the front, where she took her place by Mr. Craig.

"Nice to see you're on time today or on better time," he whispered without looking in her direction. He smiled at the children as though he were trying to hide something from them.

"What do you mean, a better time? It's not yet eight o'clock." She did the same, not looking at him, but smiling at the children. Her teeth clenched through her hissed words.

"I know. However, you are still the last to arrive if you haven't noticed. I get here at half past seven to make sure no child is here alone."

"Well, you could have told me that yesterday."

"I didn't think I would have to, being as how experienced you are in teaching. I would have thought a teacher would have already known she should be here at least thirty minutes early to make sure she is here before the children arrive."

She opened her mouth to utter another response but couldn't. He was right. She should have been here.

She closed her eyes, inhaling and exhaling a deep breath. "Fine. Tomorrow I will be here at seven in the morning. Is that better?"

He finally glanced at her. "Much better."

Before she could say another word, he stepped forward. "Class, you all remember Miss Hawthorn, don't you?"

The boys and girls all nodded and one boy, older and taller than the rest, laughed. "You mean the one who you thought was your mail-order bride?"

"And what did I tell you this morning, Hal?" Mr. Craig said.

The boy's smile faded, and he ducked his chin. "Yes, sir."

"As I was saying, class, Miss Hawthorn is a teacher, and she has come to help me for the next couple of weeks to teach you."

A little girl with white-blonde hair raised her hand.

"Yes, Sadie?" Mr. Craig said to her, pointing.

"Are you leaving us, Mr. Craig?" she asked.

"No, Sadie. I am not. I just want Miss Hawthorn's help and I think it might be good for you guys to have a new teacher just for a bit. I have wanted to evaluate how you are all doing, and this will help me do that."

The children all glanced around at each other, nodding as though to talk to each other without actually speaking.

Amelia's heart thumped. She'd never been so nervous in front of a classroom of children, and she hated the feeling. There was no way she was going to make it through a day in this schoolhouse. She needed fresh air. She needed a distraction.

"It is important to me you listen to Miss Hawthorn and do as she says. Do I make myself clear?" Mr. Craig said.

They all nodded again.

He turned toward Amelia, stretching his hand out. "They are all yours."

"Thank you." She stepped forward, taking a few deep breaths as she fidgeted with her hands. "Good morning, class."

"Good morning, Miss Hawthorn," they all said in unison.

Her knees grew weak. She needed out of this building. Now. "I'm not sure where you are in your studies. However, I was thinking . . . how would you like to go for a walk?" Along with her question, she opened up the basket in her arms

The children all gaped at her, glancing between the two teachers as though they were waiting for Mr. Craig to say something. Had he never taken them for lessons outside?

She glanced at the male teacher, who stood a little behind her, looking at the children while he shoved his hands in his pockets and shrugged his shoulders.

She turned back to the children herself. "I thought we could learn a little about the different flowers and trees that grow in Montana and get some fresh air." While a part of her thought to ask them what they thought, the other part of her told her not to care. She was the teacher. She made the rules. "Well, come on, children, grab your jackets. And you might as well grab your lunches. We can have a picnic before we come back to the classroom."

The older boy, Mr. Craig called Hal, raised his hand.

"Yes," she said to him.

"But we are supposed to work on our math lessons."

"It's all right, Hal," Mr. Craig said. "We will work on those later."

"But I need to get ahead of where I am for my tests for University." The boy's face turned a little red, and he furrowed his brow.

"It's all right, Hal. We will work on them later. Trust me, I know what your goals are. We will make it happen."

She glanced between the two, then made her way over to Hal's desk as he stood and readied himself with his jacket. He flicked the piece of clothing with an annoyance that not only she could see, but she could feel if that made sense.

"Hal, is it?" she asked.

"Yeah, what do you want?" he said dryly, a bit of annoyance hinted through his tone and, with his derision, the little girl sitting at the desk beside him slapped his arm.

"Don't take that tone with her," the girl said. "Or I'll tell Mama and Papa."

"You hush up, Isabelle. No one asked you what you thought."

"Children, please." Amelia reached out to both of them, using her hands to gain both of their attentions. "I take it this is your little sister?"

"Unfortunately." The boy rolled his eyes.

"Isabelle Porter," the little girl said, nodding her head as she introduced herself.

"It's nice to meet you, Isabelle." Amelia turned her attention back to Hal. "May I ask what math you are studying?"

"Algebra."

"All right." She clasped her hands in front of her and inhaled a breath. "Why don't you bring your book and your slate. I will give you some problems you can work on."

He glanced at Mr. Craig, who nodded as if to give his permission. The boy, still annoyed, seemed to perk up at the idea, and although there was still a slight hesitation in him, he fetched his slate, his book, and one of his clay pencils, tucking them under his arm before following the rest of the students outside.

With all of them now out in front of the schoolhouse, Amelia and Mr. Craig were alone inside.

"Are you coming with us?" she asked. Unsure of why after she uttered the words. She didn't necessarily desire his company.

"No. I'll let you handle it. As for Hal, he has certain goals he wishes to reach. If he is a problem—"

"He won't be. I've taught algebra to several children over the years. I can manage with him too."

"Well, enjoy your walk, then, Miss Hawthorn."

"Thank you. I will."

Before Mr. Craig could say anything else, she trudged outside, tucking her lunch basket tight into her waist. She inhaled a deep breath.

"All right, children. Follow me."

***

The children followed Amelia through the meadow, away from the schoolhouse and into the trees. Sunlight filtered down upon them through the branches, flecking them with light and a bit of heat with the soft rays. Amelia inhaled the deep rich forest scent as she stopped and motioned the children to circle her.

"All right, children. I want you to look around at the trees. Find one, and we will see if we can find out what kind it is in my book." She set the basket down, moving the cloth laying over the top and yanking a book out from its depths and tucking it under her arm.

While the younger children—and even some of the older ones who appeared happy with the chance of running around the forest today for school—darted off with a burst of slight laughter on all their lips, Hal remained next to Amelia. He glanced at her; his brow furrowed.

"How is this supposed to help my algebra?" he asked.

She glanced at him and smiled. "What is it you wish to be when you grow up?"

"I want to be a doctor."

"A doctor. I'm impressed, and I think you look a doctor."

A slight smile spread through one side of his lips and for a moment he straightened his shoulders, making himself taller than he already was.

"Now, I know that algebra is important for a doctor, and I'm not saying that it's not. But I also know that it is equally important to know medicinal plants and herbs. Have you been studying those as well?" she asked.

He ducked his chin, shaking his head slightly. "Not as much as I should. I know they are important. But they don't interest me as much, so I haven't. I figured I have time for all that when I complete my studies in math."

She bent down, reaching into her basket once more and

pulling out another book. "How about just for today, you set aside the algebra and," she lifted her hand as she noticed him opening his mouth to argue with her, "as I said, just for today, you study some of these." She handed him the book. "Perhaps you could look for one or two, write them down, then make a point to study them a little more in-depth. I could even request a report on them in a few days."

Hal chewed on his lip as he stared at the book for a moment, then took it from her. "You want me to find one or two?"

"Let's try two."

"All right." He ambled off through the trees, opening up the pages of the book and reading the descriptions of the pictures for a moment before bending down and running his hands across the bushes along the forest floor.

"Miss Hawthorn! Miss Hawthorn!" The other children called out. Several of them had circled a tree and were all pointing at it. "What tree is this one?"

She made her way over to the tall tree, glancing up at it. It wasn't as tall as the other trees around it, but it was a few feet taller than her. The size of it instead came from the base, and it looked like a pear with a wide bottom and thin top. It was also more of a greenish-blue than green like the others around it.

"Well, let's see what I can find in my book." She opened up the cover, scanning several of the pictures like Hal had in the herb book, searching for the right one. "Ah. I think this is it. What do you think?" She showed them the picture, and after they all nodded, she asked. "What kind of tree do you think it is?"

A few of the boys called out random names—she assumed ones they'd heard from their parents—like Ponderosa Pine, Common Juniper, or Whitebark Pine.

"That's not a Whitebark pine," one of the little girls said. "I've seen those, and they have dark pinecones that are almost black."

"Yes, that's true," Amelia said to the girl. "Does anyone else know what this tree is?" The rest of them shook their heads, so she continued. "It's a Rocky Mountain Juniper, or more scientifically known as the Juniperus scopulorum. It is a species of juniper native to the western territories. It can grow in dry soils together with other juniper species."

Isabelle raised her hand. "Miss Hawthorn, what does sco . . . scopil . . . what does that word you said mean?"

"Scopulorum?" Amelia asked, and after Isabelle nodded, Amelia continued. "It means 'of the mountains.'"

"So, it's a tree of the mountains?" Isabelle asked another question.

"Yes, that's exactly what it means. Now, shall we find another tree?"

They all nodded and took off. Amelia followed close behind them, picking her way through the dense foliage on the forest floor.

The kids screamed as they continued around, pointing at different trees. While some wanted to know more about one tree, others wanted to know more about a different one, and they all seemed to split, never agreeing on one tree over another. It wasn't until a few of them stopped and their voices all seemed to die that Amelia began watching them more closely.

"Is everything all right?" she asked the ones that were nearby.

They were all bent over, scratching at their legs and then at their arms. Some of the girls began crying, and the more they scratched, the more it seemed their whole bodies began to itch. Amelia suddenly felt her ankles itch, and she lifted her skirt slightly off the ground to check her skin. Bright red patches spread around her ankles above her shoes and the more the seconds ticked by, the more they itched and burned.

"Miss Hawthorn, what is going on?" Isabelle asked. "I can't stop itching. It burns."

More and more children started screaming about their skin burning and she spun around, glancing at the ground around her.

"Miss Hawthorn, wait!" Hal called out, trotting toward them. "You're surrounded by poison ivy!"

SEVEN

AMELIA

*B*y the time they reached the school, all the children were crying. Some more than others, and while Amelia's legs burned like they were on fire, she managed not to show she was in pain as she carried little Sadie McCray in her arms.

"What on earth?" Mr. Craig ran out the schoolhouse door, skidding to a stop as he took in the sight of the children. His mouth gaped open for a moment and before Amelia could say anything, he pointed at them. "You ran into poison ivy, didn't you?"

"I'm afraid so."

"Don't you know what it looks like?"

"Yes, I do. I just didn't think it would be around here. I never had trouble with it in Brook Creek."

"And how many nature hikes did you take while there?"

"Only a couple and it was never far from the school. The parents didn't want their children running around in the forest."

"Gee." He shoved his hands onto his hips. "I wonder why."

"Oh, just stop. I already feel awful, and I don't know what to do. We've got to help them. Once they are helped, then you can lecture me on the foolishness of my actions."

Mr. Craig opened his mouth again but shut it and instead of saying another word, he strode off, gathering the children near the schoolhouse. While he ran around to the shed, grabbing as many buckets as he could find, he told Hal to make sure all the children get their shoes and socks off, then to not only run and fetch the doctor but run around and get word to as many parents as he could.

Amelia's heart thumped as she watched the children strip down to their bare feet, then watched as Hal took off down the lane toward town. She didn't want to think about what the parents were going to say about this. They wouldn't even want her to finish out the two-week bet. In fact, she could have, in that very moment, pictured them shoving her onto the stagecoach, screaming at her to leave and never return.

Although she knew the poison ivy was not fatal and was not only treatable but would heal in a couple of weeks, that didn't erase the fact that she'd been responsible for the children, and they had come up hurt on her watchful eye.

Watchful eye. Ha. Yeah, she watched them, all right. Watched them get poison ivy.

"Now, everyone line up. We've got to wash all the skin the ivy touched right away. Come on. Line up."

One by one, the children stood near the buckets and both Amelia and Mr. Craig washed all their feet, legs, and arms as quickly as they could. The children were still miserable and as the doctor arrived and soon the parents, the sudden appearance of everyone seemed to upset them even more. They all cried as their fathers scrubbed away at the exposed skin while mothers hugged and held them, trying to wipe their tears as best as they could until they or the doctor could either apply a homemade paste—made with what smelled like oatmeal or douse them with vinegar

The whole schoolyard smelled of rotten eggs and the scent not only churned everyone's stomachs but burned their eyes a little, causing the children to cry a bit more. After the doctor went through the lot of them, most of the mothers all walked their children home. Talk of more vinegar baths and mud and oatmeal puce treatments were present on their lips. The fathers and the remaining mothers who stayed behind began circling Mr. Craig. Some stood with their arms crossed over their chests, while others had a more relaxed stance, even if they had a look of utter displeasure in their eyes.

"And just what on earth were you thinking?" one of them asked him.

"Look, gentlemen, it was all an accident—"

"Accident? I'm surprised you're trying to play this off. These children will have to deal with the pain for weeks. How could you be so thoughtless?"

"But it wasn't his fault." Amelia rushed toward them, moving into the center of the circle. "It's my fault your children were caught in the poison ivy. I wasn't paying attention to the plant life around me."

"And who are you?" another man asked. As Amelia glanced at him, she noticed young Hal and a woman next to him, standing with little Isabelle wrapped in a blanket in her arms. Amelia's heart broke. She'd caused so much pain and she wouldn't blame them for hating her.

"Well? Are you going to answer my husband? Who are you?" the woman asked. "And what are you even doing with our children? You aren't their teacher."

"I'm afraid that's my fault, Mrs. Porter." Mr. Craig stepped forward. "Listen, there's been some talk about expanding the schoolhouse to accommodate the growth in this town. And—"

"But the mayor said that was on hold until we vote on it," Mrs. Porter said. She inhaled a deep breath, glancing at her husband. "And he didn't know if it was going to happen because we don't know if we all want to pay for it right now."

"Look, I know there are a bunch of questions. The point is, it was all just a misunderstanding and I . . . well, I just thought that the children might like a change of teacher for a few days."

"But look what happened with your plan?" Mr. Porter spun toward his wife, motioning her to follow him. She took a few steps, then stopped, facing Amelia and Mr. Craig once more.

"I don't want her left alone with my children again. Do you understand me, Mr. Craig?"

Mr. Craig nodded, and as the rest of the crowd followed Mr. and Mrs. Porter, leaving the schoolyard, Amelia's stomach twisted. Although she was relieved, they didn't string her up or make her leave town, she also knew that her uphill battle to win over the children and the town just got a lot harder, and she watched them all leave, barely glancing up at them as they passed her.

As she was staring at the ground, a book came into her view, and she glanced up to come face to face with Hal.

"Here, Miss Hawthorn. Here is your book."

"Oh." She took the book, flipping it over in her hands. "Did you find any herbs or plants?"

He shook his head.

"Well, you may keep it then, if you like. See if you can find them when you are walking to and from school or out doing your daily chores." She pushed it back toward him, but he only shoved it back toward her.

"I think I'll stick to math for a bit if you don't mind."

"Of course." She took the book a second time, tucking it under her arm as he walked off, following his father back home. Disappointment flooded through her chest. She had almost brought a new level of knowledge to the boy, and now she felt like he took several steps back.

"What was that all about?" Mr. Craig asked.

"I had him studying medicinal plants since he wants to be a doctor. I thought it would get his mind off missing out on math today, which he seemed so distracted by."

Mr. Craig furrowed his brow. "That was a good idea."

"A good idea followed by a horrible one."

"Yeah. That was quite the first day you had," Mr. Craig said, making his way toward her. "Let me see your legs."

Her head whipped toward him. "I beg your pardon?"

He snorted. "Not like that. If the children were trudging through the poison ivy, then that means you were, too. Now, let me see your legs."

She inhaled a deep breath and lifted her skirt until her legs from the middle of the shin down were exposed. They burned, and she winced as the air touched her skin.

"Why didn't you wash them when we were washing the children?" he asked.

"I wanted to make sure they were taken care of."

"Yeah, I see that. But now you have blisters." He waved his hand, motioning her to follow him. "Come on. Let's get you cleaned up."

She followed him a few steps, but as he bent down, fetching a bucket to fill she stopped. "You don't have to do anything, Mr. Craig. I can wash my legs off and see to my own needs."

"You like being independent, don't you?"

"And what is that supposed to mean?"

"Exactly what the words say." He chuckled under his breath, shaking his head.

"I understand that. I meant, why does it matter if I'm independent or not? Is independence a bad thing in your mind?"

"No, it's not. I was just simply making an observation."

"Well, your tone made it sound like it was a terrible quality." She sat down on the schoolhouse steps and untied her laces, pulling her shoes off. Her hands ached from not only helping all the children with their shoes and washing them but also from the mild case of poison ivy that had gotten on her skin.

Mr. Craig opened his mouth, but shut it, saying nothing while he filled the bucket, then set it down next to her. He knelt in front of her, grabbing a bar of soap and dunking it into the water before lathering it between his hands.

He leaned in toward her, moving her skirt away. "Well, I'm sorry if my tone came across that way. I didn't mean for it to. I think independence on a person—especially a woman—is a good thing." As he finished his sentence, his hands touched her ankles.

Her heart thumped.

All thought left her, and she bit her lip—as it was the only thing she could think to do—as she watched him wash off her shins and ankles. Once they were cleaned off, he grabbed a bottle of vinegar left by the doctor to have in the schoolhouse for emergencies and poured it over her skin.

The scent hit her nose all over again, and she scrunched her face. While the burning didn't go away completely, the vinegar made it a little more bearable, and after he poured it on her skin, he returned the cap and set the bottle down next to her.

"Take that to the hotel with you and continue to pour it on throughout the night and tomorrow." He stood, grabbing the bucket, and dumping it around the side of the schoolhouse.

She glanced up at him with just her eyes. Dread filled her chest. She had wanted to hate him, and yet, she couldn't. She couldn't feel anything other than guilt and embarrassment at the moment.

"I guess I made a great first impression, didn't I?" She cradled her forehead in one hand and rubbed it with her fingers. Her fingertips were raw from all the soap, and they scratched her face.

"Yes, you could say that."

"I'm surprised they didn't ask me to leave town."

He shrugged. "They realize mistakes can happen."

"Why didn't you tell them about the bet we made?"

He shrugged again and sat down next to her. His body so close to hers rushed heat up the back of her neck and she inhaled a deep breath. She'd spent so many years telling herself she didn't want a husband—not that she saw Mr. Craig as a husband, but she couldn't help but have to face it. He was a man, and she'd spent so long telling herself not to ever consider one being in her life that she'd forgotten what it was like to be so close to one.

She could almost still feel his fingers on her legs, and the thought sent her body wanting to fidget just for something to do.

"I guess I didn't tell them because I knew if they found out they would ask you to leave. Or worse, they'd ask me to leave." He laughed. "Honestly, though, I just thought it best not to tell them."

"I'm not going to win them over, am I?" she asked as the reality of the day sat on her guilt.

"Not if you keep doing what you did today."

"May I ask you something? Why did you make the bet? I mean, do you not love this post?"

"I do love it."

"So, did you make it because you know I'm going to lose?"

He glanced over at her, giving her a half-smile as he dropped his gaze to the ground, then met hers once more. "You said it, not me."

"You are a vague man. You know that, right?"

He snorted another laugh and stood, rising to his feet as he brushed off his pant legs. "Good afternoon, Miss Hawthorn. I don't expect you or the children to feel better for at least a week if not two. So, I'm afraid there won't be any school. It's up to you if you want to continue the bet when they are all healed and back or if you just want to give up and move on."

She wanted to tell him she would stay, but before she could utter the words, she stopped herself. Another couple of weeks in the hotel meant spending more money that she didn't have, and all for a job, she wasn't sure she would get.

It was a risk.

And while the risk should have scared her—which it did a little—it also lit a small fire in her chest, and she got an idea.

An idea that could, perhaps, still win over the children and their parents.

"I'm going to stay," she said to him.

He nodded, giving her another smile that made her heart thump. How he did it, she didn't know, and there was a part of her that wished he would stop.

"That's good to know. See you around town, Miss Hawthorn." He started to walk away, but then spun around, stopping just for a moment. "Oh, if you're going to stick around, and since you wish to take my job, why don't you take care of Fletcher?"

"Fletcher? Who is Fletcher?"

"The classroom pet." He gave her a wink, and spun back around, walking off toward town at a pace that left her no time to even call after him.

A classroom pet? She thought.

But she hated pets.

EIGHT

AMELIA

Growing up, the only animal that Amelia had contact with in her parents' house was the kind she ate, and those were already butchered and ready to cook and serve. While her friends would have cats or dogs, her parents never allowed her any. Of course, when she was young, that bothered her, as she would love to play with the dogs or snuggle with the cats when visiting friends. However, the older she got, the more she realized how much work they were, and she was grateful her parents always said no.

Looking at Fletcher—a huge brown rabbit—sitting in a box with a pen in the corner of the classroom, she wished her parents were here right now, not only telling her she had to get rid of it but telling the school children no as well.

She stared down at Fletcher, and the closer she got to him, the more he flattened his ears. It had been at least a week since she'd started taking care of him, and no matter how many times she'd walked up to his cage to open it and feed him, her heart hadn't calmed one bit.

"It's just a rabbit," she had told herself each time.

Of course, no matter the species, he still scared her. Probably because the first day he attacked her, swiping his big front feet at her as she tried to hand him a carrot.

She'd run from the schoolhouse screaming that afternoon.

She'd also been tempted to open the cage door and set him free.

"All right, Fletcher. Now, I'm just going to set this carrot down. There is no need to get possessive of it. If I wanted to eat it, I would have. And I would have done it right in front of you just to be mean." She narrowed her eyes at the rabbit as she opened the cage door and reached in. Fletcher lowered his ears, crouching in the corner. His nose wiggled.

"Don't even think about it!" she screamed, throwing the carrot at him. As soon as it hit the rabbit, he jumped and shot forward, swiping his paws at her again. She fell back and scooted away from the cage. "I hate you, you filthy creature!"

"Miss Hawthorn?" a man's voice said behind her.

She spun on her rump and, looking up at Mr. Craig, she flinched. "Mr. Craig. I'm . . . please excuse my outburst." She climbed up on her hands and knees, then stood, brushing the skirt of her dress and then her hands to rid herself of any dirt she'd picked up while on the floor. "I was just taking care of the children's classroom pet."

Mr. Craig glanced down at the cage and then back at her. "Yes, I can see that. I'm sorry to have frightened you. I just didn't think you heard me come in." He pointed toward the front door of the school. She'd left it open to not only let in some light but allow the fresh air to take some of the stuffiness out. Sunlight poured through the hole.

"No, I hadn't. But there is no need to apologize. Was there something you needed?"

"I just wanted to make sure you were well enough to start school tomorrow. Most of the children are well enough that they can come back, and they've been asking too."

"They've been asking to come back? But I thought they enjoyed me coming to their houses for a few lessons."

He ducked his chin, giving an odd smile that appeared and vanished just as quick. "Well, schoolwork at home . . . it is only fun for so long before a child tires of the same four walls."

"Yes, I suppose that makes sense." She folded her arms across her chest. She'd worked so hard, making sure the children stayed on top of their lessons, traveling all around town by foot and while she was suffering from poison ivy, just to teach them. While most of the parents slammed their doors in her face, a few had allowed her inside and even though they didn't seem so happy about it, they still gave her a chance.

"Do you think you are up to teaching them when they return?" he asked.

"Yes, yes, of course. I've healed enough, and it doesn't hurt to walk."

"Good. Do you think you can help me, then?" He cocked one eyebrow, giving her a playful smile.

"Help you with what?"

He moved back over to the door and bent down, fetching several folded cloths from a basket. "I made this and thought we could hang it for the children."

She glanced through the stack of cloths. "A welcome back banner. Of course. I don't know why I didn't think of this."

"Well, not everyone can think about things like that." He winked.

Although she thought it cute, there was also a brief part of her who thought it annoying, too. Of course, he hadn't had even a hint of condescension in his tone. However, it could be there in the shadows of the words he'd chosen. Some underlying dig at her, hidden between the words.

"Let me get the stool." Choosing to ignore whatever it was she thought she heard in between what he'd said and what he meant, she made her way to the front of the classroom, grabbing the stool near the desk. It wasn't the biggest of stools nor did it look altogether that sturdy. However, she wasn't about to share any concerns with him, and she took it back to the door.

"Where do you want to hang the banner?" she asked.

"I thought outside. Above the door. What do you think?"

"I think that sounds lovely. Then the parents can see it too."

They headed outside and as he stood on one side of the door; she went over to the other, setting the stool down on the small porch before standing on it. The legs wobbled under her, and she had to outstretch both arms to gain her balance.

"Are you sure you want to stand on that?" he asked.

"Of course," she said back. "It's perfectly fine. Besides, it won't take me long to hang it." She reached out and as he handed her one side of the banner, she took it, clutching the last piece of cloth in her hand as she looked up and searched for a nail. "What do you want to hook it, too?" she asked.

"Is there a nail or piece of a board that is sticking out at all?" he asked, moving over to the other side as he unfolded the banner and searched for a spot to hang his side.

"I think there is a nail I can wrap the string around." She bit her lip as she stretched her arm as far as she could, trying to reach the nail head. Just another inch, she thought. Just another one and I should be fine. She slid her foot over to the edge of the stool, reaching out for the doorframe to help her reach just a little further.

"Almost got it," she said.

"Wait!" Mr. Craig called out, and he lunged toward her as the stool slipped out from under her.

She let out a scream and closed her eyes, trying to brace herself from hitting the ground.

A pair of arms wrapped around her, catching her before she hit.

She opened her eyes, meeting Mr. Craig's gaze. He blinked at her and heaved a few breaths. "Are you all right?"

"Yes. I am now that you caught me."

"Just in the nick of time, too." He closed his eyes for a moment, taking another few deep breaths as though for a second his own life had flashed before his eyes instead of hers. When he opened them again, his gaze met hers.

Heat washed through her cheeks, and her heart thumped. She'd been so focused on being grateful that she hadn't hit the ground that she hadn't fully thought about why she hadn't hit the ground and the sudden realization that she was still wrapped up in his arms hit her.

"Well, I guess a thank you is in order," she said, wiggling slightly to gain her freedom. Her whole body suddenly seemed to catch fire and burn and she ducked her chin as he released her and she collected her balance on her feet.

"I'm . . . I'm sorry . . . I just didn't want you to fall."

"Oh, it's all right. Thank you. I know it would have hurt if you hadn't stepped in and, well, I think I've dealt with enough pain from the poison ivy for this year. I don't need anything broken to add to it." A slight chuckle whispered from her lips as she hoped making a light joke might ease the heat building up the back of her neck.

"Maybe I should just put the banner up myself." He pointed toward the nail and then the stool, moving around her.

"Yes." She also pointed, but at him and she ducked her chin even more as she made her way toward the door. "I think you probably should, too."

Her pulse quickened, and she brushed her hand against her neck, feeling the warmth of her skin. She didn't want to think about how red her cheeks were or how flustered her voice sounded. She also didn't want to think about how his arms felt around her. Just like his touch on her legs when he was washing off the poison ivy, it had been something she'd never thought she'd want to feel and something she now wanted more than anything.

Don't do it, Amelia, she thought to herself. *Don't think about him. Don't think about that.*

She hadn't come to Lone Hollow looking for love. She'd come to Lone Hollow to teach the children. Teach and nothing else.

Teach and nothing more.

Closing her eyes for a moment, she heaved a few deep breaths, then made her way over to the desk. As she reached for her handbag, she glanced down at the rabbit, desiring for anything—even the loathing of something furry—to distract her mind.

Only the rabbit wasn't there.

The cage door sat open, and Fletcher was nowhere in sight.

"Mr. Craig!" she shouted. "Mr. Craig!"

She heard him stumble across the porch and then through the door. "What? What's wrong?"

"Does Fletcher have run of the schoolhouse when he wants?"

"Run of the schoolhouse? What do you mean?"

"I mean, do you allow him outside of his cage at all?"

"No. Why?"

"I'm afraid I left the cage open."

Mr. Craig's eyes widened. "You did what?"

"Well, I was feeding him when you came in and he had lunged at me, and I guess I just got distracted and left his cage open."

The two of them began spinning in circles, looking everywhere they could around the schoolhouse. While Mr. Craig took one side of the room, she took the other and they searched under all the desks, behind the bookcases, and even behind the coat racks and under and around her desk.

Fletcher was nowhere in sight.

As they both stopped searching and faced each other, the same thought seemed to dawn on them both and they turned their attention toward the front door that had been open the whole time.

"You don't think . . ." She let her voice trail off as she pointed toward the door.

"Oh, I think," he said. "In fact, no, I don't think. I know."

"Well, he's tamed, right? I mean, can't we just go look outside?"

Laughter shot out of Mr. Craig's mouth. "You want us to look for a rabbit outside? Because you think that in this whole time we've been here, he hasn't gotten that far?"

"Well, I don't know. Perhaps he's just eating a few bushes right outside the door. We haven't been here that long."

"I hate to say this, Miss Hawthorn, but the rabbit is gone."

"But he's the schoolhouse pet. What about the children?" What had been a spark of dread in her chest at the sight of the open cage door moments ago had now turned into an enraging blaze. "I lost the children's pet. They are going to hate me."

~

"You did what?" While most of the children just sat at their desks staring at her, the rest all shouted the same question. Their voices almost sounded like one as they took in the shock of what she'd told them.

"I didn't mean to. I was distracted by Mr. Craig, and I left the cage door open."

"So, Fletcher is gone?" Sadie McCray asked. Her eyebrows furrowed, but not in anger. Instead, it was in utter devastation, and her eyes were misted with tears.

"I can't believe he's gone!" Isabelle Porter joined in, crying with Sadie as the two girls hugged.

"I'm so sorry, children. I didn't mean to leave it open, and I'd left the door to the schoolhouse open to let in some fresh air after our long break."

"A break you caused by sending all the children out into the forest full of poison ivy." Hal sat at his desk. He was the only one who didn't look sad. Instead, he folded his arms across his chest, glaring at her with more disdain than she'd ever seen from a child in his eyes.

"I didn't mean to do that either. It was an accident. They were both accidents. Nothing more."

"You seem to have a lot of accidents. Maybe you should just go back to whatever school you came from and leave ours alone."

A few of the other boys agreed with Hal, shouting out in different tones. All with the same word. "Yeah."

She sucked in a breath, fighting off tears. If she had even the slightest chance of winning the children over after what happened with the poison ivy, it was now gone. Perhaps Hal was right. Perhaps she should leave. Only she couldn't go back to Brook Creek.

She had no place to go back to.

She opened her mouth but closed it. There was nothing she could say. No apology she could give. No reason she could explain.

The door to the schoolhouse opened and Mr. Craig came in with a box tucked under his arm.

"Good morning, children," he said. There was an odd grin on his face that Amelia almost loathed.

Why was he in such a good mood?

The children all turned their attention toward him. Some uttered a pathetic greeting in return, while others just nodded.

"What is the matter with all of you?"

"She lost Fletcher!" Hal said, pointing toward Amelia.

Mr. Craig glanced between the boy and Amelia. "Yes, I know. I was there. So, I guess you might say I lost him too."

"You didn't leave the cage open, Mr. Craig," Sadie said.

"No, I didn't. But I left the door open. However, what's done is done and while we are all sad about losing Fletcher, we have to be a little happy for him. He's now living outside, and perhaps he even met a lady Fletcher." Mr. Craig tapped Sadie on the nose, and she giggled. "Besides, Miss Hawthorn has a surprise for you, and I think you might enjoy it." He tapped on the box in his arms, glancing at Amelia, who cocked her head to the side.

She had what? She thought.

"Miss Hawthorn?" He held out the box. "Would you like to give it to them?"

She stepped forward, taking the box from him before she opened the top. Sitting in the corner were two baby rabbits, and she looked at Mr. Craig, who gave her a wink.

"Children, come around." They all listened, gasping as she bent down and showed them what was inside the box. "What do you wish to name them?"

The children all began shouting out different names, and as they took the box from her, setting it down, she backed away from them, moving over to Mr. Craig.

"Where did you get the rabbits?"

He shrugged, leaning toward her, and whispering. "I breed them. For meat."

"Oh."

"Fletcher was a baby I'd brought into the schoolhouse to teach them. Now they can learn with these two."

She inhaled a deep breath, letting it out slowly. "Thank you."

"It's no problem."

NINE

HARRISON

*H*arrison took a bite of his toast, ignoring the crumbs that fell into his plate and the crumbs that fell into his lap, landing on the napkin. The crunchy bread and buttery richness did little for his mind this morning. Neither did the coffee, scrambled eggs, or the salty strips of bacon. Normally Harrison loved Boot's breakfast, enjoying it nearly every morning—and not just because he never enjoyed doing much cooking. But this morning was a little different.

Sure, it tasted the same. But something was off and while he wanted to say it was the meal itself, he knew that would be a lie.

It was him.

He was off.

And as much as he hated to admit it, there was no cure for it.

Well, there was. But it was something he didn't know if he could do.

Miss Hawthorn had invaded his thoughts more than he cared to admit. And it wasn't just the fact that she was pretty. It was more than that. Sure, she messed up more times than not, but she meant well. She loved the children and wanted to do right by them. She was an excellent teacher and he knew that if the children and parents would give her a chance, she would do right by them and this town. Of course, with this admission came the problem of the bet.

The stupid bet he'd made first out of annoyance.

Of course, he'd made it, thinking that there wasn't the slightest possibility the children would choose her over him. And while he still felt that way, he now worried they would. Not because he worried about what kind of job he'd take in Lone Hollow if they chose her, but he worried if they chose him. That would mean she'd have to leave.

And he wasn't all right with that.

"Mr. Craig?" a voice asked next to him. Lost in thought, the sound caused him to flinch, and he glanced over to see Maggie McCray standing next to the table.

"Mrs. McCray, good morning to you."

"Good morning to you. May I sit with you for a moment?" she asked.

"Of course." He motioned toward the seat across the table and set down his fork, jogging the plate away from him just a few inches. It wasn't that he was done, but he hated eating in front of people when they weren't eating themselves. "What can I do for you this morning?"

"I was just wondering if I could talk to you about Miss Hawthorn."

His gut twisted, but he hid it behind a smile. "And what about her?"

"Well, some parents have been talking and we're all just kind of wondering why she's around."

"I told you all. The mayor is thinking about expanding the school."

"Yes, we heard. I guess some of us just thought you would be fine teaching on your own."

"That depends on how many children are in attendance. Right now, everyone seems to be doing all right. But add thirty or so more children and I'm just worried that their schooling will suffer."

"I suppose that's true." Maggie dropped her gaze to the table and her eyes darted from side to side as she furrowed her brow. It was as though she had more to say, but either didn't know if she should say it or was struggling to find the right words.

"You can tell me anything, Maggie. You and Cullen and Sadie. Your family is important to me."

"And you're important to this town. The children all love you. But they aren't sure about Miss Hawthorn. Sadie likes her all right. But Sadie likes everyone."

"Yeah, she does."

"But I've spoken to Mrs. Porter, and she said that while Isabelle is all right with having Miss Hawthorn as a teacher, Hal isn't happy. He doesn't like her, and he's voiced some concerns."

"And what has he said?"

"Well, you know they are trying to get him into a university, and he's told them he's not sure about her teaching methods and . . . well, he's worried he won't be able to get into a university with her teaching him."

"Are you saying that Hal is telling his parents that Miss Hawthorn isn't qualified to teach the children?"

"I know it sounds awful to say, but . . ." Maggie bit her lip for a moment and while she opened her mouth to answer, she shut it and simply nodded.

"I see." Harrison leaned back in his chair. He didn't know what to say. Of course, he wanted to believe she was qualified. She had said she'd been a teacher for a while, and she was posted in Brook Creek before this whole confusing mess.

A slight hint of anger bubbled in his chest. Surely, she knew what she was doing. "Well, I don't think I'd agree with that assessment. And while I never want to offend the Porters, I have to say that I think I would know about the qualifications of a teacher more than a sixteen-year-old boy."

"That's what I said to her. She didn't take too kindly to my words, but I think in the end she saw reason." A slight chuckle whispered through Maggie's chest, as though she was remembering the conversation she had with Mrs. Porter.

Of what Harrison knew of the Porters, Mrs. Porter had scared him the most. A harsh woman who always wore black, even though no one in her family had died. He often wondered if it was more for the meaning of their spirits dying every day. Her children weren't like the rest of them in town. At least Hal wasn't. Although she'd managed to rub off on her son, giving him the same sternness and a rather hard outlook on life, she hadn't managed to dampen her daughter, Isabella's sunshine. At least not yet.

"Well, perhaps I need to speak to Mrs. Porter, then. Maybe I can ease some of her concerns."

"Perhaps."

The bell above the door of the café chimed, and as Harrison glanced over, Miss Hawthorn stepped inside. Her light purple dress reminded him of springtime and he fought from smiling as he watched her bid Boots a good morning and then looked around for a table.

Their eyes met, and she inhaled a deep breath, giving him a tiny, yet hesitant, wave.

"You want to know what I think, Mrs. McCray?" he said, leaning forward and resting his forearms on the table. "I think you should spend some time with Miss Hawthorn. Perhaps if you did, and if more parents did, your concerns might disappear."

"Or not," she said.

He nodded. "Yes, or not. But I think this town should give the woman a chance."

Mrs. McCray smiled, ducking her chin for a second before looking back up. "You're right. We should." A movement seemed to catch her attention and as she glanced over her shoulder, it seemed Mrs. McCray noticed Miss Hawthorn, too. She turned back to Harrison. "You know, the town harvest dance is in a few days. Perhaps everyone could get to know her there. If someone invited her to go along with them."

"I think it would be a fine night to get to know her."

Mrs. McCray smiled as she stood, vacating the seat she'd warmed for the last few minutes. "I suppose I shall leave you to it, then. Thank you for giving me your time, Mr. Craig."

"You're welcome."

Mrs. McCray left the table, walking past Miss Hawthorn and giving the teacher not only a nod hello, but stopping for a few moments to chat. Harrison couldn't hear the conversation, but with both women smiling, he couldn't imagine it being bad. When Mrs. McCray finally excused herself, Miss Hawthorn approached his table, and he stood, setting his napkin down next to his plate.

"Good morning, Miss Hawthorn," he said.

"Good morning."

He motioned toward the table. "Care to sit?"

"Oh, I wouldn't wish to impose on your breakfast." She nodded toward the plate of food sitting near the middle of the table. A breakfast he was sure was now cold.

"You wouldn't be imposing. Please, join me."

As she sat down, Boots approached their table, taking Miss Hawthorn's order and Harrison's plate, vowing to bring it back after a few minutes back in the oven to warm everything up.

"I saw you spoke with Mrs. McCray," he said as the Irishman left their table. He grabbed his napkin and flicked it before returning it to his lap.

"Yes. She just wanted to wish me a good morning."

"I spoke to her a little this morning myself."

"I can only imagine the topic of your conversation." Miss Hawthorn's tone hinted with a slightly annoyed indifference, and she snorted a laugh through her nose.

"What do you mean?"

"I've heard what the parents are saying and thinking about me. It's a small town and some aren't as . . . what's the word I'm looking for . . . quiet about their opinion. Mrs. Porter is one of them."

He waved his hand, leaning back in his chair. "I don't know if I would give too much thought to the likes of what that woman is saying."

"I want to believe you, but it's hard to."

Harrison glanced down at the table. He knew what he had to do. Knew what he had to ask her. The problem was doing it, asking it.

"I think the town just needs to get to know you."

"You make it sound so simple."

"Sometimes things in life are simple."

"And sometimes they aren't."

While he wanted to disagree with her, he knew he couldn't. She was right. Sometimes in life, things weren't simple. Like the way he felt with her just sitting across the table from him. He didn't want to think about how many times he'd already wished that there hadn't been a misunderstanding and she'd come as a mail-order bride. But of course, he wasn't about to admit it out loud to anyone—especially himself.

"I agree. Sometimes they aren't. But you never know unless you try, right?"

"So, what do you suggest? I've already tried helping their children out when they were recovering from the poison ivy. All I got was a bunch of doors slammed in my face."

"There is a town dance coming up in a couple of days. You could mingle with everyone."

"Go to a dance by myself?"

His heart thumped. Here it was. The moment he knew was coming and yet he still wasn't exactly prepared for it. "We could go together. As teachers of the town, of course." His voice cracked, and he cleared his throat as his pulse quickened ever faster and a thin layer of sweat beaded along the back of his neck as she sat in front of him, not saying yes or no. His only hope rested on whether he'd kept his calmness enough to fool her into believing he wasn't nervous.

She blinked at him for a few more seconds, then shrugged. "I suppose we can go together . . . as the two teachers of the town."

TEN

AMELIA

*M*oonlight glistened down on the street as Amelia made her way to the town hall. It was the night of the dance, and she was even more nervous than the moment Mr. Craig had asked her to attend the dance with him.

She'd thought about those few seconds so often, the last few days leading up to the dance, they'd become burned in her mind. She didn't want to think about how much her heart had leaped when he asked her—even if he'd also mentioned they were only going together because they were both the teachers of the town.

She didn't want to remember that part of the question. The one where he played it off as something casual—even if it was.

And it should be, Amelia, she thought to herself. *You aren't here for love. And even if you desired it, you shouldn't want it with him. That would be far too awkward.*

Not to mention she didn't even know if he fancied any woman in town or if he desired to marry and have a family. Surely, if he wanted a wife, he'd have found one by now. Right?

Amelia wanted to believe he would be and since he wasn't, perhaps that meant he wasn't the marrying kind. Of course, with that thought, she also didn't want to think about the other side of that coin. Knowing he wasn't the marrying kind would be like a stab to the chest.

"I don't know why you are even thinking all of this," she whispered to herself. "You are nothing but an utter fool."

She shook her head, shaking the rest of the thoughts from her mind as she folded her arms across her chest and continued down the street toward the town hall.

Crowds of townsfolk had already begun gathering around the doors and along the streets. The chatter could be heard from around the corner, and as Amelia drew near, more and more voices and laughter boomed while music played inside. Lights flickered from the windows, shining down on the street while people cast shadows all around, looking like silhouettes in paintings Amelia had seen when she was young.

The night had a carefree feel to it, and she couldn't help but smile. Even feeling like an outsider, she wanted to soak it all in, relishing in every hint of laughter, every note of a song, and every word of conversation she heard.

She passed by one group of people and while most of them ignored her, a few nodded in her direction. The men tipped their hats, and the women smiled. She made her way through the different groups, weaving past Mr. and Mrs. McCray while they chatted with an older gentleman with salt and pepper hair who held Sadie in his arms. The little girl clutched him, wrapping her arms around his neck, and as Amelia approached them, Sadie waved her over, and the little girl climbed down from the man's arms.

"Hi, Miss Hawthorn," she said, bouncing a little on her toes.

"Hello, Sadie."

"I didn't think you were coming to the dance."

"I hadn't planned on it, but Mr. Craig convinced me to change my mind."

"Yeah, he's great at that. One day I decided I didn't want to do math anymore, but he made me see reason in that if I wanted to learn how to cook and bake like a proper lady, I would need to do math. That way of thinking changed my mind."

"And I can see why it would."

"Do you like to cook and bake?"

"Some."

"Well, I love it. Have you met Mr. Allen yet?" She pointed toward the man who had been holding her, and at his mention, he turned his attention from the McCrays to Amelia and stuck his hand out to shake hers.

"Mr. Allen Prescott. Miss Sadie here likes to call me Mr. Allen."

"A nickname I'm sure you don't object to."

He laughed along with Mr. and Mrs. McCray. "No, I do not."

"Well, I don't blame you. Not when it's given by such a wonderful little girl as Miss Sadie."

Sadie glanced between all the adults, then reached up, tugging on Amelia's sleeve with one hand while she lifted the other to her face and scratched her nose.

"Miss Hawthorn, are you my new teacher?"

"No, not new. I'm just a teacher here to help for a bit." She hated lying to the child, but she also didn't know what the truth was. "Well, I should probably head inside to find Mr. Craig. It was a pleasure to meet you," Amelia said to the man.

"You too, Miss Hawthorn."

She bid a farewell to Mr. and Mrs. McCray too, nodding toward them with a smile before she made her way to the inside of the town hall building.

Numerous tables and chairs had been set up throughout the room, and along one wall, there was another line of tables. Each one was laden with trays full of food. Crackers, sliced bread, chunks of cheese, and slices of meat decorated the first three tables while the rest were filled with trays of cookies and plates of pies and cakes. The sight of all the home-cooked delicacies whispered along her guilt. It wasn't that she didn't enjoy cooking or baking, but she had never really taken the time to learn outside of what she needed to feed herself. Always believing she would gain the skill when she became a wife and mother, she never cared much about it. But now her lack of it only further demonstrated that she'd contributed nothing to the evening, and yet attended anyway.

This wasn't a place for her to be. She wasn't a member of the town, and although she—only moments ago—didn't know what to tell Sadie, the more people who eyed her as she walked through the celebration, the more she realized she might never be.

As she made her way down to the last of the tables, she grabbed a cup of punch and took it to her lips for a sip. The band across the room had stopped playing while she had been outside with Sadie, and as Amelia took the cup to her lips for a second sip, all the men picked up their instruments, glancing at one another. One of them counted to three, and the music started up again in a beat that thumped through her chest.

The music made her smile, and she soon tapped her toes to the sounds coming from the band.

A few couples stepped out onto the dance floor and the men spun their wives around. The women's skirts spread outward from the movement, and they all laughed and smiled while others watched.

She took another sip and as she glanced to her left, a tall figure standing in a dark corner caught her attention. She looked a little more, and the figure moved into the light, revealing the man she recognized.

"Good evening, Miss Hawthorn," Mr. Craig said, stepping up alongside her.

"Good evening, Mr. Craig." Her cheeks flushed with a hint of warmth. He'd always looked handsome, but tonight . . . tonight was different. She didn't know if it was the nicer suit or the way he'd combed his hair. He looked distinguished and gentleman-like.

"I would ask you if you'd like to get some punch, but I see you already got yourself a cup." He pointed toward the glass in her hand.

"Yes, I did. It's quite good too." She took another sip, keeping the glass at her lips a little longer than she needed just for a distraction.

"So, I was thinking," he said, leaning toward her a bit more to be heard over the music. "We are probably past all the formal greetings. I mean, I don't think it would be bad for you to just call me Harrison. Everyone else does."

"Oh. All right." She paused, inhaling and exhaling a deep breath. "Well, if we are past it, then I suppose you can call me Amelia."

He nodded, smiling at her. "I've always liked that name. Amelia."

Her name purred off his lips and, for the first time in her life, she, too, liked her name. Not that she hated it all the other times. But hearing him say it. It was different. If any of that made sense.

They both continued to watch as more and more couples came together and started dancing around the room, and as more of the townsfolk came into the town hall, the room—more crowded—closed in around them.

Amelia kept sipping on her glass of punch, and as she took the last sip, her heart thumped.

Now what, she thought. Of course, she could get another glass of punch, continuing her quest to distract her mind. But she also knew that too much of the tart, but sweet lemonade mixed with some other fruit punch on an empty stomach was just the right combination for a stomachache. Something she didn't want to experience tonight.

Just set the glass down and keep watching, she told herself.

As she turned to set the glass down, Mr. Craig turned too, taking it from her before she could reach it out toward the table.

"Would you like to dance?" he asked.

Her knees grew weak with his words and although she tried to take in a deep breath, she couldn't.

"I beg your pardon?" It was perhaps the most foolish response in the history of responses, but it was all she could think to say.

"I asked if you would like to dance?" He offered a smile and motioned toward the dancefloor.

"Oh . . . um . . ." Just say yes, she thought, you know you want to. "Yes. I suppose that would be nice."

He set both his and her glass down on the table before outstretching his hand to motion her out onto the dance floor.

Her hands trembled as he took one in his and she rested the other on his shoulder. She wanted to close her eyes but knew she shouldn't and as his arm wrapped around her and his hand touched the small of her back, she leaned into him. Her heart pounded, and the beat drummed in her ears. She wanted to hold her breath, but she knew she couldn't. Not to mention, she didn't want to miss a second of inhaling his intoxicating cologne.

Front step, back step, and sidestep, they continued around the dance floor through the first song and then a second, before the songs ended and they broke apart to clap for the band. Harrison motioned for her to follow him back over to the punch bowl, and he grabbed himself a glass, asking her if she wanted another one. She shook her head.

"Have you talked to many people tonight?" he asked, taking a sip.

"Not really. I met Mr. Allen. Sadie introduced us."

"That's nice. You should probably try to mingle at least a little, though."

"I have to say, I would have thought that you wouldn't want me to do that." She chuckled, more to herself than out loud.

"Why do you say that?"

"Well, what happens to you if I make friends in this town? Or charm the parents enough that they choose me over you to teach their children? Don't you like your post? Your job? The children?"

"Of course, I do."

"Then why would you be all right with me taking it all away from you?"

He opened his mouth for a moment without saying a word. Finally, he shook his head and blinked. "I . . . I don't know why I'm doing it. I suppose it's just in my nature to help people."

"It's in your nature to help people take your post?"

A glass shattered against the ground behind them, and they both spun as Hal ran off, leaving the mess he'd made behind.

"I'll get a mop," Harrison said, and he trotted toward the other side of the building while Amelia shoed everyone away from the area and bent down to pick up the larger shards of broken glass. Punch was spattered across the floor and the pieces of glass slipped in her fingers. She carefully picked up as much as she could, and they rattled in her palm as she stood and laid them all down on the table. As she finished, Harrison returned with a mop and a bucket of soapy water, and he sopped up what punch he could before taking care of any other glass shards that were too small to pick up.

"Thank you for your help," she said, wiping her hands off after he finished and shoving the mop and bucket under the table.

"I wonder what got into Hal. Doesn't seem like him to just run off like that." Harrison glanced around the room.

As he was looking, movement caught the corner of Amelia's eyes and she turned just as Mrs. Porter stepped up on the stage where the band was.

"Excuse me, everyone!" She shouted.

People around her silenced and although there was a lot that hadn't heard her, the others who had tapped those around them still talking on the shoulders to quiet them down. It wasn't long before she had everyone in the room looking up at her.

"I just thought you would all like to know the scheming that has been going on under our nose. I know that most of you have expressed your displeasure with the new schoolteacher, who has suddenly appeared and hasn't left for reasons we did not know. I'm here tonight to tell you those reasons. It seems that Mr. Craig has a bet with the woman. If she can win over the town and the children, then she can have the teaching post."

Amelia and Harrison looked at each other, then at the crowd, who had all spun around toward the pair.

Harrison held up his hands. "There is no scheme, Mrs. Porter."

"Really? So, you are calling my son a liar? Because he heard every word of your conversation just now with Miss Hawthorn."

"All right. There was a bet," Harrison said.

The townsfolk in the room gasped and glanced at each other.

Harrison looked around at them and then at Amelia. His brow furrowed, but not in anger. It was as though he was full of nothing but the deepest regret. Like he was about to do something he didn't want to do. "But you have to know I only did it because I knew she couldn't win. I adore your children. I wasn't about to give them up."

"Then why make a bet at all?"

One half of Amelia battled against the other. While she felt shocked and betrayed, she also felt this overwhelming need to help Harrison. To protect him from the crowd's wrath. This whole mess had gotten out of hand and while she hadn't started it, she had taken a role in it. She'd let her pride and competitiveness impede what mattered most: teaching the children.

She wasn't a good teacher.

And she didn't deserve them or this town.

"It was my bet," she stepped forward. "I made it. He didn't. He only took it, and I am certain he only did because I egged him on." She paused for a moment, clasping her hands. Her fingers fidgeted with one another. "He loves your children, and he is the best for them. I shall pack my bags and be on the next stagecoach out of Lone Hollow."

Although Harrison tried to stop her, she weaved past him and darted for the door, letting it slam behind her. She didn't know why she'd done what she had or what was going to happen. But it didn't matter. The only thing that mattered was that she got out of this town as soon as she could.

ELEVEN

AMELIA

A knock rapped on the door to Amelia's hotel room. "Amelia? Are you in there?" Harrison asked. "Please, open the door. I need to speak to you."

Amelia stared at the door for a moment. While she wanted to tell him to just go away, there was a part of her that wanted to just remain silent, letting him believe she'd either already left or wasn't there.

"I know you're in there. Mr. Stoneridge, the owner, said you hadn't come down yet and the stagecoach won't be here for another hour. Just please open the door. I want to talk to you."

"Go away, Mr. Craig. I don't wish to talk to you," she finally said.

"Please."

"Just go away."

An envelope slid under the door, and she moved over, bending down to fetch it. Half expecting a letter when she opened it, she was shocked to find money instead.

"What is this money?"

"The mayor asked me to give it to you."

"But what is it for?"

"It's two weeks' pay for teaching the children."

"But I didn't teach them."

"Yes, you did, and you should be paid for it. Now, please, let me in."

She took the money from the envelope and folded it before shoving it into her handbag and moving closer to the door. While she wanted to give the money back, the fact that she had nothing to her name stopped her. She had spent every dime she had on the hotel room, and now that she had to leave . . . well, how was she supposed to find a way to Butte without any money? The fact was, she couldn't. She'd have to take what the mayor gave her.

She pressed her forehead to the wood and closed her eyes as she fought tears. "There's nothing left to say between us, Mr. Craig. Just let me leave."

"I can't do that."

"But you must. Do you understand me? I have nothing here, and you need to let me leave."

"And what about us?"

"Us? There is no us. Just . . . please go. I have to pack, and I can't do it with you here."

She backed away from the door and moved over to the bed, covering her ears as he knocked several more times, demanding she open the door. When she didn't, he gave up, abiding by her wishes, and as she darted over to the window to look down on the street, she saw him leave the hotel, glancing up at her before he walked away.

~

*I*n the hour that passed while she waited for the stagecoach, Amelia had cried in her room for most of it. But for the last several minutes, she knew she would need to wait downstairs, and so she made her way down to the first floor and settled into the chair near the door to wait. A few people were meandering about the lobby. Other guests who were checking in or just seemed to be content with chatting with the owner of the hotel, Mr. Stoneridge, about one thing or another, and another man who sat statue-like in another chair. His head was tucked down to his chest and his hat was pulled down to cover his face.

He didn't move nor look up when Amelia sat down. However, she caught him a few times watching a little girl who was with a couple of the guests as she ran around the lobby, pretending as though she was a horse.

He's probably one of those types who hates children, Amelia thought to herself.

Her theory went proven for a moment until the girl bumped into the man's legs and while Amelia expected an outburst from him, he simply looked up at the girl and smiled.

"Excuse me, Sir," the girl said.

"Well, it's all right, little lady. You were just playing." He studied the girl, looking at her from her shoes up to the top of her head. "Aren't you a pretty little thing? What are you trying to be?"

"A pony."

"A pony? Don't you want to be a horse? Horses are bigger and can do more than ponies."

"But I like ponies."

"Yeah, I guess that's understandable. Say, how old are you?"

"Seven."

"Seven. Well, you're practically a young woman."

Amelia's brow furrowed at the man's comment. How was a seven-year-old practically a young woman? And why would a grown man say this? She glanced at the two, then at the parents who were still chatting with Mr. Stoneridge.

"So, do you have a pony at home?" The man asked. He lifted his head a little more and Amelia caught his face. Long and thin, in an oval shape, his eyes were close together and his long black hair draped his face.

"No. I don't," the girl answered. "Papa said he might buy me one if we move to Lone Hollow, though."

"Well, that's nice. I hope he can get you one. I don't have a pony, but I have a horse outside. He's brown. Would you like to see him? I'll even let you ride him if you want."

The girl stepped back from the man. She blinked at him a few times, then looked at her parents. "Pa said I'm not allowed to go with strangers."

"Oh, we aren't going anywhere. Just outside the hotel."

Amelia's heart thumped as she listened to the conversation. What on earth was this man trying to do? Or thinking?

The little girl looked back at her parents, then down at the ground. She kicked her toes on the ground as though she were kicking a rock.

"You want to know a secret, too?" The man asked, leaning in toward the girl. She leaned away, but it didn't deter him. "I just got this horse a few nights ago, and I haven't named him. How about I let you name him?"

"I can name him?" She blinked at the man.

"Of course, you can. You can name him anything you want, and I'll keep the name forever. But you should see him before you name him."

The little girl stepped back away and glanced at her parents a third time. "I don't think I should go unless my Pa and Mama go too. But thank you."

Before the man could say anything else, she trotted off. He watched her for a moment, then slunk back down in his chair, covering his face with his hat.

Amelia clutched the handle of her bag, trying to take several deep breaths to calm herself as she leaned back in the chair. She didn't want to replay what had just happened in her mind, and yet, she also wanted to figure out what it was she just saw. She didn't know what she was going to do, whether it would have been to say something, follow them outside, or tell the girl's folks—perhaps she'd even have done all three. But she was glad the girl decided not to go, and as the couple left the hotel with their daughter, she blew out a breath.

"The stagecoach is here for those who need a ride," Mr. Stoneridge said, announcing it over the room before he made his way to the door, holding it open for anyone leaving.

Amelia stood, watching the man for a moment before she turned and left. Part of her was thankful he wasn't following behind her, as she didn't know how she would feel if he'd climbed in with her.

Sunlight beamed down on the street as she crossed the porch of the hotel, waiting for the man and woman standing in front of her to board the coach before her and for the driver to take her bags. She wanted to look around at Lone Hollow one last time, and yet, didn't. She didn't want to face the heartbreak she knew would come with it. She'd spent so much time longing for this town, and then finally being here . . . and being with him.

She closed her eyes at the thought of Harrison. A small part of her wished she would have spoken to him—at least one last time—but she knew just as much then as she did now that it would have been pointless. Nothing he could say would change anything and it would have only made the situation worse.

No, it's better this way, she thought, better for you to leave and find another town to teach.

A town that needed a teacher and would love to have her help them with their children.

Not like Lone Hollow.

"May I take your bags, Miss?" the driver asked, holding out his hand.

She handed him the two bags and after he hoisted them onto the top of the stagecoach, she climbed inside the carriage and sat in the seat across from the couple. They smiled and nodded, and after she returned the greeting, she ducked her chin down, dropping her gaze to the floor. She didn't wish to be rude, but she also didn't wish to speak with the couple either. The thought of casual chitchat was nothing short of torture at the moment.

$\sim$

*I*t wasn't long before the driver finished and had climbed up into the driver's seat. Amelia felt the stagecoach lurch underneath her and the wheels began rolling down the street. She both wanted to look out the window and didn't at the same time, and although she fought hard against it, she allowed herself one last look, watching the hotel fade in the distance as they rolled out of town.

"Are you heading to Butte?" the woman asked her.

She glanced at her for a moment and nodded, hoping the lack of words would be enough of a hint to them. She didn't want to be bothered.

It didn't seem to work.

"That's nice. We are too. We were visiting family in Lone Hollow. Were you here just on holiday? Visiting someone, perhaps?" The woman blinked at her, waiting for an answer.

She said nothing again, only nodded, and with her silence this time, the woman finally took her hint and turned her attention toward her husband. The two of them ignored Amelia, finding conversation in each other instead of the companion on the stagecoach, who just wished to be left alone.

$\sim$

*S*unlight beat down on the stagecoach as it rolled through the meadows and trails of Montana. Birds chirped from the trees, and there were times Amelia could see them from the window, see their wings flap as they fluttered from branch to branch. She'd always had a love and hate relationship with birds. Loved their beautiful songs and how they always seemed to make the day cheerful, as though they passed along their happiness to whoever would listen to them. And yet, sometimes, like today, when there was little happiness to be found, they were almost annoying. This was where the hate came in. Of course, hate was such a strong word. Perhaps dislike was better. In the end, Amelia supposed it didn't matter.

A horse galloped past the window, and Amelia sat up, leaning into the back of the seat. She heard a few shouted words, and the stagecoach came to a halt.

"What's going on, dear?" the woman asked her husband.

"I don't know." He leaned forward and moved out of his seat, opening the carriage door as he poked his head out. "There seems to be someone who stopped the stagecoach."

"Well, we know that," his wife shot back with an annoyed crispness. "But why have they stopped it? They aren't robbing us, are they?" With her question, she lifted her hand and clutched her throat.

Amelia's heart thumped. She hadn't had that kind of thought until the woman had said something.

"I don't think they are. It looks to be a sheriff who stopped us. Don't know any lawmen around here that would rob a stagecoach." The husband opened the door a little more then stepped out, vanishing for a moment as he walked up to greet the man on the horse.

While the wife remained in her seat, pressing her back against the carriage as she inhaled and exhaled deep breaths and fanned her face, Amelia stuck her head out of the window, trying to catch any part of the conversation she could.

She couldn't hear anything, though, and the curiosity got the better of her. She climbed out, making her way in the direction the husband had gone.

"You're more than welcome to check the stagecoach, Sheriff Bullock. But I never saw a little girl board," the driver said. He looked at the husband. "Did you see a little girl around before we left?"

"No, I didn't. But I will ask my wife."

As the husband trotted back to the carriage door, Amelia stepped forward. "What's wrong, Sheriff?" she asked.

The Sheriff looked down at her. His big blue eyes narrowed, and he moved his horse to face her. The big grey gelding towered over her. "Are you Miss Hawthorn?"

Amelia sucked in a breath. "Yes, sir. I am."

"A little girl is missing from Lone Hollow. Her mother thought maybe you might know something about it."

"I beg your pardon?"

"The little girl who is missing is Isabella Porter. Do you know her?"

"Yes, I do. I . . . I was the teacher that helped Mr. Craig for a couple of weeks. I know the girl, but I know nothing of her missing."

The sheriff nodded toward her, then turned to the stage-coach driver. "Jasper, I'm going to have to ask you to return to Lone Hollow. Your passengers can take the one leaving in a few days and tell them I'll cover the hotel bill for their inconvenience."

"Yes, Sheriff Bullock."

The sheriff moved his horse forward a few more steps toward Amelia. "And Miss Hawthorn, when we get into town, I'm going to need a moment to speak with you."

"Of course, Sheriff."

TWELVE

HARRISON

"I know she took her!" Mrs. Porter screamed in Harrison's face as the woman bordered between anger and terror.

"No, you don't, Mrs. Porter. You can't be sure she took her. Why would she?"

"As punishment."

"Punishment for what?"

"For having her run out of town."

Harrison took his hand to his forehead, rubbing his fingers along his skin. He pressed as hard as he could, hoping the pressure would ease the pounding that had already begun. He hated headaches, and today's would prove one of the worst ones he'd ever felt.

"But you didn't run her out of town. She left by her own accord. Mrs. Porter, I know you didn't care for Miss Hawthorn, but trust me when I say she is not a bad person. She never would have kidnapped your daughter. She loves the children she teaches. Probably more than I do."

Mrs. Porter backed away from him, shaking her head. Tears

streamed down her cheeks, and she buried her face in her hands. "I know she took her. I just know it."

As Mr. Porter wrapped his arms around his wife, more and more townsfolk gathered around them. They whispered amongst themselves, and while Harrison should have wished to know what they were saying, he was also glad he couldn't. Of all the mistakes Amelia had made in this town, he knew she wasn't capable of kidnapping. No matter how she felt about the town or Mrs. Porter. Not once had he heard her utter an ill word toward anyone in this town, and he knew she was innocent.

He just knew it.

"Mr. Craig?" Hal asked. "May I help ask people around town?"

"Of course, you can." Harrison laid his hand on the young man's shoulder. "Why don't you go get Boots to help you while we wait for Sheriff Bullock to return?"

The boy nodded and spun, running off toward the café while Harrison watched.

As word continued to spread, more and more people fanned out. Not only looking around but asking everyone they knew in town who hadn't heard the news if they'd seen the girl. Ranchers returned from their homes, only to leave again as they began their searches in all directions from the town, and businesses closed their doors to help stop the girl from leaving their stores if she was hiding in one of them. They all searched every inch of their buildings. Even Mr. Stoneridge demanded every hotel door be opened so he could check all the rooms.

Little Isabelle Porter was nowhere to be found.

And Harrison didn't know what else to do.

All that was left for them was to wait for Sheriff Bullock to return with the stagecoach.

~

AMELIA

*A*s the stagecoach pulled into Lone Hollow, Amelia noticed the crowd and her heart thumped. She didn't even wait for the coach to come to a stop before she opened the door and climbed out. The movement knocked her off balance, and she stumbled a few steps before regaining it. She rushed toward Harrison in the middle, but before she could reach him, Mrs. Porter rushed toward her, shoving her.

"Where is she?!" Mrs. Porter screamed in her face. "Where is my daughter? What have you done with her?"

"I haven't done anything with her."

"Liar! Do you hate me that much? That you would take her from me. I know she's with you. She's in the stagecoach right now." Mrs. Porter moved around Amelia and headed toward the stagecoach, searching through it all as she screamed her daughter's name several times.

"Mrs. Porter, I don't hate you. I do not know where Isabelle is. I don't have her."

Mrs. Porter backed away from both the stagecoach and Amelia and glanced at the Sheriff, who shook his head as though to answer a question she didn't ask.

"Well, if she doesn't have her, then who does?"

"We don't know, Mrs. Porter, but we will find her." The sheriff climbed down from his horse and made his way through the crowd toward Harrison, who had already started making his way to Amelia.

"Any word?" the sheriff asked him.

"None."

"All right. I'm going to ride out and see if I can find anything." He slapped Harrison on the shoulder, then moved around him, raising his voice for everyone to hear. "If any of you men wish to ride out and help, then I suggest you get your horses. We can fan out in all directions."

Most of the men in the crowd ran off, grabbing their mounts from different tie posts around the hotel, and those of the ones that remained started chatting to themselves about where they each could start looking.

"Hello," Harrison said, shoving his hands in his pockets as he walked up to Amelia. He dropped his gaze to the ground and cleared his throat. "I guess that sounds funny to say that, given everything going on."

"Yeah. I don't know what else could be said. So, what happened?"

He shrugged. "No one knows. Mrs. Porter was at the dress shop, and Isabelle asked to go outside for a moment. When Mrs. Porter came out, the girl was gone. She thought she'd just run off to find Hal who was at the general store, but he hasn't seen his sister."

"So, they assumed I took her?"

"I told them you didn't, and I knew you didn't."

"Thank you for that. And you're right, I didn't."

"Everyone has been looking all over town. No one has found anything, and no one saw anything."

Amelia glanced around the town and all the people who had stayed behind instead of going with the sheriff on horseback to search. People were looking around the buildings, checking the rain barrels and water troughs with their arms, sticking them down in the water as though they thought the girl had climbed into one. Of course, some of them were big enough to fit the girl but full of water, there was a scarce chance of them finding her in any of them.

Mr. and Mrs. Porter watched from the hotel porch along with Pastor Duncan, who stood with them, praying over the couple and their daughter. While Mr. Porter had his arm around his wife, rubbing her shoulder, she had her face buried in her hands and Amelia could hear her sobs. Her own words of prayer were muffled in her hands. Amelia had cared little for the woman while she was in Lone Hollow, but feelings aside, she never wished this kind of pain on the family.

"Has anyone checked the schoolhouse?" she said to Harrison. "Perhaps she wanted to visit the baby rabbits."

His eyes narrowed, and he shook his head. "It was the first place I looked."

"Is there any other place she loved to visit?"

"They've checked them all, and Mrs. Porter doesn't understand how she could just run away. She's gone outside when they've shopped before, but she's always stayed around the store. She's not one to wander off. She never has been in my class, either."

"So, you think someone took her?"

He inhaled and exhaled a deep breath. "I think so."

"But who would do that? Who would take a little—" As Amelia was about to finish her sentence, a couple walked past her with a little girl between them. Each one of them had a hold of her hand and Amelia recognized them from the hotel that afternoon while she waited for the stagecoach to arrive. It was the same little girl who had been trotting around the lobby pretending to be a pony.

And the same little girl who had been talking to that man.

The stranger who made Amelia uncomfortable.

"Ponies," she whispered to herself.

"What?" Harrison cocked his head to the side. "What about ponies?"

She gaped at him, then sucked in a breath, clutching her throat. "I know."

"You know what?"

"I know who took her."

THIRTEEN

AMELIA

"*W*hat do you mean, you know who took her?" Harrison trotted after Amelia, following her as she rushed into the hotel lobby.

"Where is he?" she asked.

"He who? The man who took her?"

She glanced around, not searching for the stranger with the low hat but for Mr. Stoneridge. It was a wild guess that he would know anything, but perhaps he would.

"No, Mr. Stoneridge." Before Harrison could say another word, Amelia darted up the stairs, calling for the hotel owner a few times before she found him still searching through rooms.

"What can I help you with," he asked, looking up from checking under a bed.

"Earlier this afternoon, a man was sitting in the lobby. He had on a black hat and black hair. Do you remember him?"

The hotel owner's eyes squinted as he thought, and he rubbed his chin with his hand for a moment before it appeared as though it hit him.

"Yes, I remember him. I asked him if he wanted a room for the night, but he said he was just passing through."

"Did he mention where he was headed?"

"Brook Creek. He said he had a cabin outside of town, and he didn't need anything from me. I was kind of glad to see the man leave. He was making the guests uncomfortable." Mr. Stoneridge paused for a moment, then his eyes widened, and he blinked several times. "You don't think . . ."

"Yes, that's exactly what I think. He was trying to get a little girl to go outside with him to see his horse when I was here this afternoon." She turned to Harrison. "One reason I was happy to leave Brook Creek was because of the people moving into the town. All the families were leaving, and other types were moving in. The town wasn't as safe anymore."

"All right. Well, let's head there. Maybe we can find him and find her before it's too late."

❧

It had been years since Amelia was last on a horse, and while she wanted to believe she could still sit in a saddle as good as she had in her youth, she also couldn't deny she was not in practice.

And by the way, she flopped all over the saddle, out of balance too.

After the pair had rushed the stairs, they not only left word with Pastor Duncan for Sheriff Bullock as to where they were going, but Amelia had borrowed the pastor's horse. He was a gentle gelding with a smooth rocking gait, but even with his smoothness and kind nature, she still struggled, and by the time Brook Creek came into view, she felt relieved.

Or at least a little.

Sure, it was nice to see the town, for it meant she could get out of the saddle. But at the same time, it was still a town she never wanted to see again, and she was there for a horrible reason.

"Mr. Stoneridge said the man mentioned a cabin outside of Brook Creek. Do you know of one that it could be?"

She shook her head. "I stayed mostly in town—especially toward the last few months of living here."

"Do you know of anyone still living here that could help us?"

"The mayor."

"Let's go find him."

Any hustle that was once a part of the town of Brook Creek had long since died out as people left town. The streets, now barren, held a hollow feeling to them. It was worse than when she left only a couple of weeks ago, with most of the businesses looking as though they were shut down. Most of the buildings had busted-out windows and broken doors, and a sense of abandonment hinted through the dirty town. Only a few men walked along the sidewalks, and while most of them ignored the newcomers, a few stopped and stared, watching Harrison and Amelia as though they were waiting for the pair to do whatever it was the men thought they would do.

Harrison halted his horse outside the closed café and climbed off before moving over to Amelia's horse and helping her down.

He looked around. "Is there an office for the mayor?"

"It's just down that way."

"Wait here. I'll see if I can find someone that will follow the law around here."

While she stuck close to the horses, Harrison wandered off down the street. She watched him for as long as she could, and when he vanished from sight around the corner, her breath quickened. She glanced around, spying the men who had noticed them and were now staring at her. A woman. All alone. What had Harrison been thinking of leaving her here?

What had she been thinking about coming here?

She closed her eyes for a moment and clenched her teeth at

the thought of why she'd come. She came here looking for a little girl who was probably scared for her life.

And a lot more scared than you are right now, she thought to herself.

She glanced around again just as another man came from the saloon. His long black hair draped his face, and even though he'd pulled his hat down low, she recognized him from the hotel in Lone Hollow.

There he was.

Her heart thumped.

She looked around him, but there was no sign of Isabelle, and she watched him approach a chestnut horse, checking the girth before he made his way to the tie post to untie the reins. He was about to leave, and if she didn't do something, they would miss their chance. She had to stop him. She had to do something. If they missed this chance and this man had Isabelle, they might never find her.

She reached around, untying her horse before leading him over to the man.

"Excuse me, sir," she said.

The man flinched and spun around to face her. His eyes grew wide. "What do ya want?" he asked. His voice was high-pitched and nasally, like he spoke more through his nose than his mouth.

"I'm sorry to bother you. I . . ." She bit her lip. She had to play this right, charm him with kindness and not let him onto the fact that she was asking for a specific reason. "Well, I was wondering if you could point me to a nice place where I might stay the night. My horse . . . he stumbled, and although he seems to be walking all right, I would like for him to rest. I happened upon this town and thought you might know of a place I could stay."

She offered a smile, not knowing how the man would react.

His brow furrowed for a moment, then his head jerked back.

"Haven't seen a woman around these parts in a few days. They all moved out of town."

"Oh, well, I don't live here. I was just passing through."

"You expect me to believe you were riding alone?"

"And why wouldn't I? I'm a . . . a dressmaker, and I couldn't wait for a stagecoach. I'm designing a dress for a wealthy client, and she couldn't wait. So, I decided just to go alone."

"A dressmaker, huh?" He eyed her again, tracing her body with his gaze from her feet to her head. "And you said, for a wealthy client?"

"Yes, that's right."

He turned his attention back toward his horse, checking the other side of the girth before untying the second rein and throwing it over the horse's neck. "Well, there ain't no hotel in town anymore. You're welcome to come to my place."

Amelia's breath quickened as heat rushed up the back of her neck. She wanted to glance over her shoulder to look for Harrison but didn't want to act suspicious in any way.

"That's very kind of you. Where is your place?"

"It's just a few miles outside of town. Your horse can rest and . . . well, I don't have much for food, but I have a place for you to rest too."

"That sounds lovely, and I have some food on me for the trip so that I won't be needing much. Just a place to rest and for my horse."

Her body trembled as she made her way back to the horse's side and stuck her foot in the stirrup. She hoisted herself back into the saddle, glancing down the street toward Harrison's horse. It was still tied, and he was nowhere in sight. A voice in her head screamed at her to stay and wait while another said this was her chance to find Isabelle, and if she didn't take it, the girl would be lost forever.

You'll think of something, she thought to herself.

⟨∾⟩

*T*he entire way toward the man's cabin, she thought of different ways to get away from him. Perhaps she could even just go as far as finding the cabin, only to tell the man she would not stay and then return later. She knew she'd been reckless. Knew she'd been foolish. But she also knew that somewhere there was a little girl who needed her help, and as they finally approached the cabin, something told her not to leave, but to stay and find the girl.

"You have a nice place," she said, pulling her horse to a halt. She glanced around at the cover of the trees that blocked out most of the sunlight, giving the place the feeling that it was nearing night time.

"It serves its purpose. I don't think I'll be here much longer."

"Oh, are you moving out of Brook Creek?"

"You could say that. I've got some things lined up and once the payday comes in . . . I'll be heading to California." He gave her a smile that caused an itch to move down her skin, and he reminded her of a weasel. As cute as the creatures were, he was something different. There was something sinister about him, and while she'd gotten a glimpse in the hotel at Lone Hollow, it was magnified in the middle of nowhere.

They both climbed off their horses, and as she tied hers, he began untacking his. "You can put your saddle on the fence if you want, then turn him loose in the corral."

"Oh. Um. I think I'll just leave him tacked up. It won't do him any harm, as long as he can sleep and rest his leg."

He studied her for a moment, then shrugged and finished with his horse, letting it loose in the pen before he motioned for her to follow him into the cabin.

Her knees grew weak and as her mind fought her legs to keep moving toward the danger, she held her breath and closed her eyes for a moment as she stepped across the front porch of the cabin.

She glanced over her shoulder, not only hoping to find Harrison riding up to the cabin, but perhaps Sheriff Bullock too. Of course, just Harrison would be all right, too. Just as long as she wasn't alone. She knew why she'd gone with this man, but still knowing the reason didn't help her feel any better. What if she'd been wrong? What if he hadn't taken Isabelle?

"So, what is this payday you speak of?" she asked, clinging to any question she could use as a distraction for not only herself but hopefully for him.

Just keep him talking, she thought, if he keeps talking, then perhaps she could buy herself some time.

He opened the door and motioned her inside. "I'm glad you asked, lady. Because that's what I wanted to show you."

She stepped inside and gasped as Isabelle lay on the bed, bound and gagged. The little girl's eyes widened, and she began screaming even though there was a rag in her mouth.

The door slammed behind Amelia, and she spun as the man pressed himself against the door, blocking it.

"What's the matter? Did ya think I didn't recognize ya from the hotel in Lone Hollow? Watching me while I was trying to talk to that little girl."

"If you knew I came for the girl, then why did you bring me here?"

"Because this is your fault."

"My fault?"

"That family . . . in Lone Hollow. I'd been following them for quite some time. I knew how much they were worth. Now you better just hope that the ransom I collect for you and her will cover what that family would have paid for the other girl." He pointed to Amelia and then to Isabelle.

"You don't need to ransom me. I'll pay you what you need. How much do you want?"

"Five thousand dollars should get me to Mexico just fine."

Amelia clutched her throat. "Her family doesn't have that kind of money. No one in Lone Hollow does."

"Well, you better hope they figure out a way to get it. For her and you."

Amelia glanced all around the cabin. The windows were shut and locked, and the only door was the one the man was standing in front of.

"Don't ya be doin' what I think ya are doin', either."

"I beg your pardon?"

"Don't think ya are goin' to be escaping somehow." He moved his coat away from his hip and yanked a gun from his holster. "I got no problem shooting both of ya and leaving town to find another girl to take."

Amelia backed away from him as he waved his gun around. She sat down on the bed, and as Isabelle sat up and reached for her, she wrapped her arms around the girl.

"It's going to be all right," she whispered as Isabelle started crying. She didn't know if she could believe her own words, but she knew saying them would help.

FOURTEEN

HARRISON

*H*arrison peeked through the bushes, moving the branches slightly to the left while he gazed upon the cabin. Amelia had gone inside with the man only moments ago and it took all the control he had in him to not run after her.

He couldn't, though. Not until he had a plan. He didn't know how many other men were in the cabin and he didn't know how many weapons were in there.

After discovering that the mayor of Brook Creek had left the town, he had returned to the horse, planning on not only telling Amelia about the mayor but also planning to tell her he'd also decided they needed to find a place to hunker down and wait until Sheriff Bullock and some men showed up. What he hadn't planned on was to return to find Amelia across the street, climbing on her horse, and following some strange man away from town.

A stranger that had now led her—and without knowing Harrison—to this cabin that Harrison now watched.

He didn't want to think about why she'd done what she had. He didn't know if she knew the man—although he greatly doubted it because she didn't wait for Harrison—or if, perhaps, he wasn't a bad man, and he knew of Isabelle's whereabouts. Again, though, if he was a good guy, why wouldn't she have waited for Harrison?

Nope, he thought to himself, *everything pointed that this was the man she believed responsible, and she went with him to find Isabelle, knowing that if she'd waited for Harrison, she would have missed her chance.*

It was a dumb way to go about something, especially for a woman, but he understood why she did it.

He just wished she hadn't.

With a slight groan to his breath, he glanced up at the sky. The sun had already begun to set, and the sky had turned into a purple and pink brilliance that he could see through the trees. He didn't want to be in the woods at night, and yet, he knew he could sneak around the cabin easier, perhaps he could even peek inside the windows.

As the sun dipped down, lower and lower, the once purple and pink sky dimmed into a light grey that darkened into a deep black. Owls hooted from the trees and the birds that were once chattering to one another in an almost obsessed manner went silent. Replaced with the chirps of crickets and the occasional croak of a frog.

The darker the forest became the closer Harrison inched toward the cabin, and it wasn't long before he reached one of the outside walls and stood next to it, pressing his back against the wood. He inhaled and exhaled several deep breaths, trying to calm the anxious swirl in his stomach. His heart raced and he closed his eyes for a moment before sliding himself along the wall toward the nearest window.

The glass was dirty and had a film on it that blurred the inside of the cabin. Still, with the grit and grime, he could somewhat see Amelia sitting on the bed, talking to one man standing over her. She had Isabelle wrapped in her arms.

Harrison twisted his body, moving in a few different angles to try to catch sight of anyone else inside with them. He couldn't find any other person though, and as he set his attention back on the man and Amelia, the man lunged forward toward his captives. Both Amelia and Isabelle screamed, and the last thing he saw before he spun and ran for the door was Amelia kicking out at the man, trying to defend herself from his advance.

It was the image that Harrison pictured in his mind as he dashed for the front door, slamming his shoulder into the chunk of wood, and shoving it open.

The door flung into the wall behind it and the man spun. Knocked off balance by Harrison's sudden burst through the door, the man stumbled backward then brushed his jacket to the side, trying to grab the gun holstered at his waist.

Harrison lunged forward, wrapping his arms around the man, and the two of them flew a few feet before landing on the ground with a thud. Double the size, Harrison overpowered the man using his weight to hold him down. The man wiggled underneath, still reaching for the gun.

"Get out of the cabin," he shouted at Amelia. "Get out now. Take Isabelle."

~

AMELIA

*W*ith Harrison's shouted order, Amelia scooped Isabelle up in her arms and ran for the door. The men rolled around, struggling with one another on the floor. She wanted to stop and help but knew she had to secure the girl.

Once outside, the colder air hit her exposed skin and she trembled as she laid the girl on the ground.

"It's all right. I've got you now. Let's get you untied." In the haste of the situation, her fingers fumbled with the ropes tied around the girl's hands and feet, and while she managed to get them undone, it wasn't without the casualties of a couple of her nails and a few scratches to the girl's legs and wrists. Once untied, she led the girl over to the horse, helping her to climb on first before climbing on herself. She wasn't about to leave Harrison there, but should the man come after them, she wanted to be ready to flee.

A gunshot rang out from the house and she froze.

The night seemed to go silent around them and Isabelle buried her face in her hands. The girl trembled against Amelia's chest.

Although Amelia wanted to breathe, she couldn't, and she closed her eyes for a moment, opening them as Harrison stumbled out of the front door. His shirt was stained with red and as he hit the porch, his balance gave out and he went down to his knees.

Isabelle screamed and Amelia threw her leg back over the horse, jumping down before she ran to him. By the time she reached him, he'd gotten back to his feet.

"Are you . . ." No matter how much she'd wanted to finish her sentence, she couldn't.

"It's not mine," he said, motioning toward his shirt. "I wasn't shot. He tried . . . but I took it from him."

Amelia buried her face in his chest, sobbing as he wrapped his arms around her.

"It's all right. It's all over," he whispered.

They both stood there for a moment before they turned to Isabelle who was still sitting on the horse. Tears streamed down the little girl's cheeks, and she had her arms wrapped around her middle as though to hug herself. Amelia didn't know if the girl shivered more from the cool night air, the shock of the whole ordeal, or both, but she guessed it was the latter.

"Can you take me home?" she asked, her tiny voice cracked with her words as she cried.

They both nodded.

~

*B*y the time they were a little way outside of Brook Creek, several horses galloped toward them. Sheriff Bullock led the pack, and holding a lit torch, he halted the group as he reached them.

"The man who took her?" he asked Harrison after hearing the story.

"Dead." Harrison hooked his thumb over his shoulder, motioning toward the makeshift stretcher attached to his horse. The wooden poles had left marks in the trail behind them.

The sheriff nodded, telling two of the men to get down, untie the stretcher from Harrison's horse and tie it to their own. He then asked another two men to ride back to Lone Hollow to tell the Porters they had Isabelle and were on their way home.

"I know a lot of people out looking for you who will be mighty pleased to see you," he said to the girl, giving her a wink.

The ride back to Lone Hollow had taken longer than Amelia thought. Of course, it had been the same distance, but the pace was slow and while she finally felt like she could take full breaths, knowing the danger was over and the outcome had been everything they could have hoped for, the girl still clinging to her only made her think about the damage that was done. She knew not of the nightmares this girl would have, but she could guess, and she wouldn't wish them on anyone, much less a girl of Isabelle's age. Perhaps one day they wouldn't haunt her, but how long it would take, Amelia didn't know.

And she didn't want to think about it.

As they neared Lone Hollow, several more torches and lanterns lit up the streets and Mr. and Mrs. Porter ran for them.

Mrs. Porter screamed for her daughter and as they drew near, Amelia climbed off the horse, helping the girl down so she could run to her parents. The three of them embraced and with Hal following a few feet behind, they all collapsed in each other's arms. Everyone cried even the other townsfolk who had come out to see the girl come home.

"Thank you," Mrs. Porter said to Harrison and Amelia as they approached the family. "Thank you so much."

Harrison raised his hands for a moment then pointed to Amelia. "It wasn't me. It was all her. She recognized the man and went after him. I only came into the situation after the fact."

Mrs. Porter released her daughter and hugged Amelia. Tears streamed down her cheeks and glistened in the light of the lanterns. "Thank you."

"Of course," Amelia whispered. Although she didn't know if it was the right thing to say at this moment, it was all she could think of.

FIFTEEN

AMELIA

"So, is it unanimous, then?" The mayor stood at the head of the room, holding a gavel in his hand. He hovered over the podium as he glanced over all the townsfolk sitting around him. "Do you all agree with Sheriff Bullock that Mr. Craig is best suited for Deputy Sheriff of Lone Hollow?"

"Aye," the town responded.

Amelia glanced over at Harrison sitting next to her. He met her gaze and reached for her hand, clutching it in his. He smiled.

"Then it's settled. Sheriff Bullock, you may swear in your deputy as you see fit. Now, onto the next matter. With Mr. Craig leaving the school, it seems we are in search of a new teacher." Mayor Jackson glanced over to the Porters. "Mr. and Mrs. Porter, you mentioned you had something to say?"

They both nodded and stood. Hal stood too, and Isabelle jumped from her seat. She didn't run to her mother, though. Instead, she ran to Amelia and climbed into Amelia's lap. Amelia wrapped her arms around the girl, hugging her.

"We wanted to extend our sincere apologies to Miss Hawthorn for the things we said." Mr. Porter glanced at his wife. "And we also want to say that we'd be honored if Miss Hawthorn would stay in Lone Hollow and teach our children."

The rest of the town all nodded and agreed with different yeses answered and hummed words.

"Miss Hawthorn?" Mr. Porter asked. "Would you want to stay in Lone Hollow and be the teacher?"

"Of course, I would."

The mayor smacked the gavel down on the podium again. "If the town agrees, then that matter is settled. Is there any other business anyone wishes to discuss?"

Harrison stood up, raising his hand. "I have something, Mayor."

"What is it, Mr. Craig?"

Harrison moved out from in front of his chair into the aisle. He spun around, sticking his hand in his pocket. "Well, Mayor, it's actually about the housing for the teacher."

"Oh, yes." The mayor ducked his chin for a moment. "Well, I suppose we can let Miss Hawthorn stay in the hotel until you find a place of your own. Then she can move in."

"Well, that's the thing. I was kind of hoping we could just find a place of our own."

A few of the women around the room gasped and Isabelle wiggled from Amelia's lap. A smile beamed across her face, and she giggled.

"Our place?" Amelia asked Harrison. She cocked one eyebrow.

"Well, if you'll have me." He knelt on one knee, taking his hand from his pocket and holding up a gold band in between his finger and thumb. "Amelia Hawthorn, would you do me the honor of being my wife?"

She smiled as a slight flush of heat warmed up through the back of her neck. She hadn't come to Lone Hollow to find love. But that was what she found.

Love. Total and complete love.

The kind that makes the heart thump at just the thought of the person. Every time she looked at him, he weakened her knees, and she couldn't wait to spend the rest of her life with him. "Of course, I will."

He slipped the ring on her finger and leaned in, kissing her before he pressed his forehead into hers. "And to think this all happened because of a total misunderstanding."

THE END

DID YOU LOVE HER MAIL ORDER MISUNDERSTANDING?

READ BOOK FOUR OF THE BRIDES OF LONE HOLLOW

She's trying to flee her family who are wanted bandits . . .

He's the Sheriff out to protect his town . . .

What happens when he finds out about her past? And what happens when that past catches up to them?

ORDER OR READ FOR FREE WITH KINDLE UNLIMITED

HER MAIL ORDER MISCALCULATION

Turn the page for a sneak peek at Book Four in the Brides of Lone Hollow Series.

ONE

There's a sense of peace that comes in the night. When all the world is asleep and quiet. Cora Bennett loved the night. Nighttime was the only time she had to herself. Nighttime was the only time she could not only hear the thoughts in her head without interruption from her brothers but dream the dreams she had. She wanted more out of the life she'd lived for the last nineteen years, and it was in the nighttime she could not only hope for it but pray for it.

Dear God, she would say every night. *Please help guide me to find the life of my dreams, the love I desire, and the freedom I long for. I pray this in Jesus' name. Amen.*

It was the same prayer she whispered night after night.

It was the same hope she lived day after day.

Her eyes fluttered open as the dark grey light filtered through the window of the cabin. The sun still had hours before rising, and as she sat up, she glanced around. Her heart thumped. Her two brothers and mother were still asleep. If she hurried, she could run to Ashley's house and return home before they woke up. They were all up late last night. They should sleep in.

Should being the key word.

Hopefully.

She slowly removed the blankets and slid out of bed, grabbing her boots before she snuck outside. The cool air made the hair on her arms and the back of her neck stand, and she slipped on her boots, tiptoeing across the porch and to the barn where she saddled her horse.

The moon still shone down through the trees, flecking the forest floor with a ghostly shade of white. Shadows played off the dark places and between the brush, allowing the creatures still prowling for food at night a chance to hide.

Cora continued to ride as the sky lightened, the stars vanished, and an explosion of pink and purple replaced the plain grey. She didn't know how many times she'd taken this route in all the years her family had lived in the cabin. Of course, most of those times had been at night while her family slept. She wasn't allowed out during the day—or at least out alone—and, certainly, wasn't allowed to have friends.

"Friends could discover secrets or could be told secrets," Cora's mama always would say, and Cora had enough secrets to fill a water trough. While Ashley knew some of them, she didn't know all, and Cora only kept it that way to protect Ashley, not herself.

If Mama knew about the girl down the road . . . she shook her head, shaking away the thoughts.

Cora didn't want to think of what would happen. She didn't need the lectures. She also didn't need the punishment.

As Ashley's house came into view, Cora stopped and lifted her hand to her mouth, letting out the sound like the hoot of an owl. She waited a few seconds before doing it again, waiting a little longer the second time. Before she could do it a third, another sound responded, and she smiled as she cued her horse to move closer to the house.

A lantern bounced toward her, and as Ashley held it up to

her face, she waved to Cora, letting out a deep sigh as the two met at the fence.

"I wasn't sure if you heard me," Cora said.

"And I wasn't sure if you heard me."

The two girls giggled, and Cora slid off her horse. "I don't have much time." She bit her lip. The whole ride to Ashley's, she wanted to hope that a letter from Mr. Wyatt Bullock—the Sheriff of Lone Hollow—waited for her, but she also couldn't deny there was a little fear that she would once again arrive to find nothing. "Did anything arrive for me in the last few days?"

Ashley smiled and nodded, yanking an envelope from the belt around her waist. "This came yesterday. I wanted to get word to you about its arrival, but I didn't know how." She handed Cora the envelope, and Cora took it. "Is it from him?" she asked.

Cora glanced at the name etched on the front and nodded. Her hands trembled as she flipped it over in her hands and stuck her finger in one end, ripping the top open. She withdrew the paper and unfolded it, reading the words so fast she had to read it a second time to make sure she didn't miss a single one.

"Well?" Ashley asked. "What does it say?"

"He wants me to come to Lone Hollow." Cora's heart fluttered as she read Wyatt's words a third time. They had been everything she'd been longing to hear—or read—from him the whole time they had been corresponding.

"It's so exciting." Ashley bounced on her toes for a moment, then she stopped, and her smile vanished. "What are you going to tell your mother?"

If Wyatt's words had been everything Cora had hoped for, Ashley's words had been everything Cora had dreaded, and while she wanted to give her friend an answer, the fact was that she couldn't. And not because she didn't want to. But because she'd never thought of what it would be. Of course, she wanted to know. Or at least wanted a life where it wouldn't even be a question. But she hadn't thought of it because she was scared. Scared of the answer. Scared of the truth.

"I don't know."

"Are you going to tell her?"

Cora didn't know which was worse—Ashley's first question or her second.

"I don't know that either."

Sickness swirled in Cora's stomach as an itch crawled through her skin. She shoved the letter back in the envelope and tucked it into her pocket. "But I should get back to the house before they know I'm gone."

"All right." Ashley bit her lip, then reached out, grabbing Cora's arm. "If you leave, will you at least write to me?"

Cora leaned toward her, wrapping her arms around her friend in a tight hug. "I will."

"Promise?"

"Promise."

~

By the time Cora made it back to the cabin, the sun had already risen enough to light the sky in a brilliant splendor of blue. White puffy clouds peeked through the trees, and Cora held her breath as she untacked her horse and crossed the porch of the cabin, slipping her boots off first so the heels wouldn't make noise on the wood. She turned the doorknob and opened the door slowly, peeking her head in.

They were all still asleep, and it wasn't until she slipped back into her bed and covered herself up that her mama finally woke and sat up, growling as the sunlight filtered in through the windows.

"How is it morning already?" Mama asked.

"I don't know, but if you don't shut your mouth, I'll shut it for you," Mitch, Cora's oldest brother, said, rolling over. He threw his pillow at Mama, and it smacked her in the face.

She let out a louder growl and threw it back. He had moved, though, and the pillow landed on Denny's—Cora's second older brother, the middle child of the three of them—head. He flung it off, sitting up.

"What in the world was that for?" His brow furrowed, and he shot Mama a stern glare.

"I wasn't aiming for you," Mama said, pointing toward Mitch. "I was trying to hit your brother."

"Well, have better aim next time." Denny rubbed his face and ran his hands through his hair as he yawned. "It's far too early to be awake. I need some coffee."

"So get up and make some yourself. Who do ya think I am, your servant?"

"No, but you are our mama. You could do some things for us, ya know?"

Without a word, Mama slid out from under the blanket on her bed and made her way to Denny's. He smiled as though he thought she would give him a pat on the back, but instead, she leaned over and slapped him on the back of the head.

"You're a grown man, and I'm done raising you. Get your own coffee. Slacker."

"Slacker? Do you know how much I did last night? Moving all those bags of flour and sugar that we stole from that house down the road."

"You mean the three bags?" Mitch sat up, throwing his own pillow at his brother. He had more force behind this throw, though, and the pillow smacked Denny in the face.

Cora's heart thumped. Ashley had mentioned that her Pa was talking about supplies missing. She didn't want to think that her family was the reason. However, knowing that it was them didn't surprise her. It was just another reason she wanted to protect Ashley. Even if her family had already stolen from the girl's family, if they knew she knew them, it would be worse—way worse.

"I didn't see you carrying any," Denny said to Mitch. "In fact, I didn't see you do anything last night."

"What are you talking about? I kept watch, and we almost got busted too because you made so much noise."

Denny threw the pillow back at Mitch just as hard as the latter had done. Mitch didn't take the taunt too kindly, and he lunged for Denny's bed. The two of them collided, and after both of them got a few punches in, they rolled off the bed, falling to the floor with a thud.

"Both of you stop it right now." Mama stomped across the room, kicking the two of them until they both stopped and were holding their arms and legs in pain from her punishment.

"You don't have to kick us that hard," Denny said, rubbing his shoulder.

"Apparently, I do. Now get your butts off the floor and make your own coffee."

Cora finally sat up. Done listening to all of them, she wiggled out of bed. A slight groan whispered from her lips. "I'll make the coffee."

"It's about time the princess woke up," Denny said as she passed them.

"And what is that supposed to mean?"

"Nothing, princess."

Her two brothers laughed at the one's joke, and while Cora wanted to retort something witty, she also knew it was pointless. Pointless to say, anything witty around them. Pointless to dig at them. Pointless to even make sense around them.

Everything with those two was pointless.

She shook her head, making her way over to the kitchen to fill the kettle with water. Then, fighting a yawn from her early morning adventure, she put the kettle on the stove and opened the door, tossing in a chunk of wood to reignite the dying flame.

Mama also moved around the house, fetching a newspaper from the counter and sitting down at the table. The chair legs scraped along the wood floor, and the entire table wobbled from her weight.

She unfolded the paper, scanning the headlines. Cora tried to peek at the black words written on the white pages, but every time she tried, Mama moved the paper.

"This is it, boys," she said, finally setting it down on the table. She pointed her finger down toward one article and tapped it with her nail. "This is the payday we're looking for. Right here. This will get us to Mexico."

"Mexico?" Cora froze with her hand on the bucket of water she'd used to fill the kettle. "What do you mean? Why are you talking about Mexico?"

"Because that's where we're going, Princess," Denny said. He finally climbed up from the floor and grabbed his boots from under the bed, slipping them on.

"We decided last night." Mitch got up off the floor, too, still rubbing the back of his head where Mama had kicked him. "Didn't we tell you last night when we came home?"

"No, you didn't tell me when you came home last night." Cora rested her hands on her hips. "Mama, is it true? Are we going to Mexico?"

"Seems like that's the plan." Mama didn't take her eyes off the paper, and she spoke in a mundane tone as though so bored with the conversation, she wasn't listening.

"But why do we have to go to Mexico?"

"Because that's where we decided to go." Denny stood from the bed and made his way over to the stove, shoving her aside before he bent down and fetched a sack on the floor. He threw it on the table before opening it and yanking out a loaf of bread from its depths. He took it to his lips and bit off a huge chunk.

Mitch stood and rushed over, taking the loaf from him and

ripping off a bigger chunk with his hands. "Don't hog it all. This is one of the last ones we have."

"So, just have Princess make us some more today. We got the flour."

"Bread needs yeast cakes, dummy." Mitch took a bite, chewing it as though he hadn't had a meal in years. "Don't you know anything?"

"So, get her some yeast cakes."

"Oh, yeah, just get her some yeast. With what money?"

Denny shrugged, turning his attention back to his half of the loaf. A slight growl rumbled through his chest.

"Both of you just hush about the bread. Soon we will have more bread than we know what to do with." Mama pointed to the paper again, tapping it harder with her finger. "This is what we need to focus on."

The brothers both leaned forward, reading the headline. Cora didn't know why they did, though, and she moved around them, looking over their shoulder.

"I don't know why you're looking," she said. "You know you both can't read."

Mitch shoved around her, letting out a *humph* noise as he headed over to the stove to pour himself a cup of coffee. Denny just left the table and gathered his boots, hat, and shirt, putting them all on before sitting on the edge of his bed.

Cora read the headline:

NICHOLAS VANDERBILT TOUR THROUGH MONTANA
TO INCLUDE BUTTE AND THE SURROUNDING TOWNS

Cora glanced at Mama and shrugged. "I don't understand."

"And I didn't think you would." Mama rolled her eyes and moved away from the table, fetching her boots from under the bed. She sat on the edge of the frame and slipped her feet inside.

Cora watched Mama, waiting for her to explain further.

When she didn't and instead headed toward the door, Cora called after her. "Mama? What does that article mean?"

Mama grabbed the doorknob, twisting it until the door popped open. She heaved a deep sigh, turning toward Cora. Her eyes fluttered in annoyance. "It means a wealthy man is touring the country with this wealthy wife. Wealthy people travel with money, and wealthy wives travel with jewels. We rob the stage-coach and head to Mexico. Now. Stay here while your brothers and I prepare to leave this place for good."

"Do we have to do this?" Cora took a few steps toward Mama as Denny and Mitch jumped to attention and followed Mama to the door. The three of them gaped at her momentar-ily; then, her brothers started laughing.

"She can't be serious, can she?" Denny asked Mitch.

Mitch shook his head, then wiped his nose. "I'm not sure, but I think she is."

"Do we have to do this?" Denny mimicked her question in a baby-like voice.

They both laughed again.

"Hush, you two," Mama shouted. She pointed at the door. "Go tack up your horses. Now."

As they darted through the door, she smacked both of them on the back of the head. After they vanished outside, Mama turned to Cora.

"I don't know what I'm going to do with you sometimes, Cora. But to answer your question, yes. We have to do this. I want out of Montana. I've wanted out ever since your father was murdered."

"He wasn't murdered."

Anger flared in Mama's eyes, and she held up her finger. "He was murdered!" She paused. "We're doing this, Cora, and we're doing it my way. If you cause any problems for me, I swear once we get to Mexico, I will sell you to the first man who wants you."

Before Cora could say a word, Mama slammed the door. The force nearly knocked over a few bottles sitting on a shelf on the wall.

Cora's eyes filled with tears, and she blinked them away before they streamed down her cheeks. She didn't want to go to Mexico. She also didn't want to rob another stagecoach. The only thing she wanted to do was travel to Lone Hollow to marry Mr. Wyatt Bullock.

"And that's exactly what I'm going to do," she whispered to herself.

TWO

*I*n all the years Wyatt Bullock had been sheriff, he'd never felt so on edge. It washed through him like a river washing over the rocks. Of course, with all the robberies in Pinewood and Sterling, towns near Lone Hollow, and word of a wealthy man and his wife taking a tour through the state, how could he not be?

"Did you find any tracks?" Deputy Sheriff Harrison Craig asked as he rode up and halted his horse near Wyatt's.

"A few. Headed out that way toward Brook Creek. I knew that town would become a problem after what happened with little Isabelle Porter, but I didn't expect this. I suppose as long as they stay there, though I can't do much about it." Wyatt sat in the saddle, scanning the horizon for any early morning movement. The only thing he saw were a few rabbits hopping in the grass. His horse sneezed, and they froze.

"Have you spoken to Jasper? Has he seen anything running the stagecoach through the area?"

"He hasn't." Wyatt shook his head, remembering the last conversation with the stagecoach driver. "But he told me he's keeping his eye open. He's also prepared to protect himself and the stagecoach if necessary, especially when he's carrying the likes of Nicholas Vanderbilt and his wife. Those two will be a welcomed prize to the criminals living in Brook Creek should they get wind of the tour. I never knew why the press would think to share such news in the newspapers, but anything to sell a paper."

Harrison's eyebrows furrowed. "Well, let's hope a situation doesn't come from that."

"I'll second that."

The two men cued their horses to walk down the trail, and they stayed quiet for most of the ride back to Lone Hollow. Not only was Wyatt trying to listen for any odd sounds, but he also had something else on his mind. Something other than a band of bandits who've decided to cause trouble.

"Something wrong, Sheriff?" Harrison asked.

"No. Why?"

Harrison shrugged. "I don't know. You look like you've got something on your mind."

"I do. We have a band of bandits running around the area."

"No, I know that. I don't know why I just got the feeling there was something else going on. I can see that I'm wrong, though. Forgive my asking."

"It's not a big deal—certainly, nothing to apologize for. I suppose I wasn't exactly truthful with you. I do have something else on my mind. I just . . . well, I'm not sure I wish to discuss the matter."

"I understand."

Wyatt repeated Harrison's words inside his head. He knew the newly engaged man would probably be the best one to talk to about what was going on in his mind, but still, he didn't know if he could talk about it. Did men talk about things like this? About love and marriage and women? And even if men did, did a sheriff?

It felt odd to think about it all, yet he couldn't help but feel the urge to say something.

"How is Amelia doing?" he asked, going for a more passive way around the subject.

"She's as lovely as ever. We've started on the wedding plans. She wants to keep it small." He chuckled. "Honestly, between you and me, I think she would just invite the children and no one else."

"Maybe that's what you two should do, then."

Harrison glanced at him, then smiled and nodded. "Maybe."

The two men continued to ride down the lane toward Lone Hollow, and the early fall morning, so crisp, brought both a refreshing chill and the hint that winter would be upon them before they knew it.

"Do you ever wonder what would have happened if there hadn't been a misunderstanding about Amelia's school post?" Wyatt asked again, taking a passive way around the topic.

Harrison glanced at him. A flicker of confusion at the questions seemed to furrow in his brow as he answered. "What do you mean?"

Wyatt shrugged, and his chest tightened. He didn't want to explain his vagueness, and he hoped Harrison would have just known what he wanted to say even if that was foolish for him to think.

"Well, I suppose I meant . . . it was fortunate that the misunderstanding had happened. I suppose God knew what he was doing." Wyatt glanced up at the sky, wishing the bright ball of light would burn him into dust at this very moment.

Harrison shifted his gaze toward Wyatt and smiled. "You mean with the problem of not a lot of women living in Lone Hollow?"

Wyatt's heart thumped. "Well, yeah. I suppose I mean that."

"It is a problem I think most men have in this town." Harrison chuckled. "I don't know if you know, but the misunderstanding with Amelia came when I wrote to a man named Mr. Benson. He's a marriage broker."

"I'm aware of Mr. Benson." Wyatt spoke before thinking about whether he wanted to say those words, and he clamped his mouth shut.

"So, you've been in contact with him?"

Although Wyatt didn't know if he wanted to answer the question, and yet at this point, he thought it foolish not to. He had already admitted so much. Why not just have the conversation he was scared to have? Maybe if he did, he wouldn't fear it so much.

"Yes."

"And do you want to tell me about her?" Harrison smiled and wiggled his eyebrows.

"Her name is Cora."

"And . . ."

"And she lives with an aunt and an uncle in Butte. She is a kind lady, and although she seems proper, there also seems to be a bit of wildness to her. I can't put my finger on it; I just get the notion it's there."

"Sounds like you like her, and she is perfect for you. Have you talked about her coming to Lone Hollow?"

Wyatt sucked in a breath. They'd done more than talk about it. Or he supposed he had. He'd brought it up out of the blue in one of the letters, and she had, much to his shock, been open to the suggestion.

"Actually, I have sent for her. She should arrive today."

"Today?" Harrison's mouth gaped for a moment, and then he blinked several times. "I . . . wow."

"Yeah. Wow. I guess that is the first time I've said it out loud."

"So, she's arriving today. And what are you going to do?"

Wyatt's eyes widened at Harrison's question. Of course, he had written Cora the letter, finally asking her to come to Lone

Hollow, but even with penning the words, he still hadn't thoroughly thought about what would happen when she arrived.

Marriage would happen, he thought to himself.

Was he ready for that?

He thought he had been. Why else would he have penned the letter asking her to come? No, he was. He was sure of it. But still the thought of her walking down the aisle . . .

He gulped at the pictured image in his head.

"I suppose I will put her up in the hotel and get to know her more than I already have."

"And the wedding?"

Wyatt shrugged, inhaling and exhaling a deep breath. "I guess we will start plans for one, too."

ORDER OR READ FOR FREE WITH KINDLE UNLIMITED
HER MAIL ORDER MISCALCULATION

WAGON TRAIN WOMEN

Five women headed out West to make new lives on the Frontier find hope and love in the arms of five men. Their adventures may be different, but their bond is the same as they embark on the journey together in the same wagon train.

CHECK OUT THE SERIES ON AMAZON!

Turn the page for a sneak peek at book one, Her Wagon Train Husband.

ONE

ABBY

*E*veryone loves adventure.

Well, almost everyone.

Abby had to correct herself on that point. Her parents didn't like adventure much. Neither did her three older sisters. They liked being home. They liked being in a place they knew. They didn't enjoy the thrill of the unknown or the sense that the world could open up right under their feet.

Of course, that wasn't an appealing thought. For surely that would mean death. And Abby didn't like the idea of that. She just liked the adventure.

Yeah, she thought to herself. I don't like that.

Abby heaved a deep sigh as she walked along the path around the lake. It was a favorite pastime for her and one she enjoyed nearly every day. Well, every day that her parents and sister's stayed in their country home. When they were in the city . . . well, that was another story. She would often sneak out of the house and head to the park. Even if she had to be careful about being seen, she would still try to get in a little walk in the trees and sunshine. Wasn't that what Spring and Summer were for? Perhaps even Autumn? Winter surely not, although she couldn't complain too much about those months. For she loved the snow too and would enjoy it until her fingers and nose turned red, and her skin hurt.

Something about nature called to her like a mother calls to a child when they want them to come home or to the table to sit down and share a meal. She loved everything about it. The smell of the air, the sound of the birds, and the leaves rustling in the breeze. The feel of the sunshine upon her skin and how it felt as though her body tried to soak it all in like a rag soaks up water.

The outdoors made her feel alive.

Much like the sense of adventure did.

And the two, she thought, went hand in hand.

"Aammeelliiaa!" She heard a woman's voice call out in the distance. Her name was long and drawn out and sounded as though the woman—her mother—calling had her hands up against the sides of her mouth.

Her heart thumped. She couldn't be caught coming from the direction of the lake, and yet, there would be no chance to sneak around to the other side of the stables without being seen. Her mother called for her several more times, and as she tried to round the stables, appearing as though she came from a different direction, she heard her mother's foot stomp on the front port.

"Abby Lynn Jacobson! And just where have you been?" Her mother raised her hand as if to stop her from answering. "Don't even tell me you were walking around that lake all by yourself."

"All right." Abby squared her shoulders. "I don't tell you that."

Her mother's eyes narrowed, and she pointed her finger in Abby's face. "You listen to me, young lady; you will not go flittering off again. Do you understand me? You have far too many responsibilities in this house to do anything other than what you're supposed to be doing."

"But sewing and cooking and cleaning are just so boring. I want to be outside."

"Outside is no place for a woman unless they are out there to hang laundry on the line or gardening. Both of which you need to be doing too." Her mother continued to wave her hands around the outside of the house, pointing toward the laundry line and the fenced garden around the back of the house. Clothes already hung on the line, and they moved in the breeze. "Your sisters certainly don't spend any time fooling around outside."

"That's because my sisters are married and have husbands to look after."

"And you will have one too. Sooner than later, now that your father has made it official."

"What do you mean?" Abby jerked her head, and her brow furrowed.

"Mr. Herbert Miller is on his way over to the house this afternoon."

"Why?" Although she asked, she wasn't sure she wanted the answer, nor did she believe she would like it.

Her mother shook her head and rolled her eyes. "To finalize the agreement and plans to marry you and take care of you, of course."

Abby sucked in a breath and spit went down the wrong pipe. She choked and sputtered, coughing several times while she gasped. "I . . . I . . ." She coughed a few more times and held out her hand until she regained composure. "I don't want to marry him."

"That's not for you to decide. He comes from a well-to-do family and intends to provide a good life for you. Not to mention we could use the money." Her mother clasped her hands together and fidgeted with her fingers as she glanced around the home. It was still in good shape for its age, but even

Abby had seen some of the repairs it needed, and she knew her parents couldn't afford it. "I dare say he's the richest young man out of all your sister's husbands. You will have a better life than any of them."

"And you think I care about that?"

"You should. It's well known around St. Louis that the Millers have the means. There are mothers and fathers all over the city who would love to have him for a son-in-law. You're going to have quite the life, young lady."

"But is it quite the life if it's a life I don't want?"

"How can you not want it? A husband. A nice home. Children. It's all you've wanted."

"No, it's all you've wanted. And it's all my sisters have wanted."

"Oh, spare me talk of your dreams of adventure." She rolled her eyes again and wiggled her finger at her daughter. "There is plenty of adventure in being married and having children. Trust me."

"That's not the kind of adventure I want, Mother."

"It doesn't matter what you want, Abby. Your purpose in life and in this family is to marry and have children. If you're lucky, which it looks like you are, you will marry a nice man with means. You should be happy. You could have ended up like Mirabel Pickens." Mother brushed her fingers across her forehead. "Lord only knows what her parents were thinking marrying her off to that horrible Mr. Stansbury on the edge of town. He's at least twice her age and hasn't two pennies to rub together. Of course, he acts like he does, but honestly, I think the Pickens family gives them money." Mother fanned her face with her hand. "Now, go upstairs and change your dress. Fix your hair too. He'll be here within the hour."

Before Abby could protest any further, her mother spun on her heel and marched back across the porch and into the back door of the kitchen. Abby stood on the porch. Part of her was too stunned for words, yet the other part wasn't shocked at all. She always knew this day was coming. It just had come a little sooner than she thought it would, and although she had thought of a few excuses or reasons she could give to put it off, with Herbert on his way to the house, she didn't know if any of them would work.

Scratch that.

She knew none of them would work.

Her parents had their eyes set on the young Mr. Miller for a while, and there wasn't any reasoning they would listen to that would change their minds.

It wasn't that Herbert—or Hewy as he once told her she could call him—was a dreadful young man. He wasn't exactly what she would call the type of man she would hope to marry, but he was nice. He was taller than most men his age and skinner, and he wore thick glasses that always seemed to slip down his nose as he talked. He was constantly pushing them back up, and there were times Abby wondered if he ever would buy a pair that fit better or if he enjoyed the fact they were a size too big. Like had it become a habit for him and one he liked.

She remembered how distracting it had been at the Christmas dance last December that her parent's friends hosted at their house. Every few steps, he would take his hand off her waist to push them back up his nose, and he would even miss a step here and there, throwing them both off balance because he had to lead. He'd even stepped on her foot once or twice.

Her toe throbbed for days after that party.

No. She simply could not marry him. She just couldn't.

If her mother wouldn't see reason, perhaps her pa would.

She marched across the porch and into the house, making her way toward his office and knocking on the door.

"Come in," her pa said from the other side, and as she

opened it and moved into the room, he glanced up from his desk and smiled. "Good afternoon, Abby."

"Well, it's an afternoon, but I'm not sure it's a good one."

He cocked one eyebrow and threw the pencil in his hand down onto a stack of papers on the desk. "What has your mother done now?"

"She's informed me that Mr. Herbert Miller is on his way to the house to finalize an agreement for my hand in marriage." She paused for a moment but then continued before her father could say a word. "Father, I know you aren't going to accept it. Right?"

"And what makes you say that?" He glanced down at the papers on his desk as he blew out a breath.

She knew where this conversation was headed. She'd seen this reaction in him she didn't know how many times in her life. When faced with a question that Pa didn't want to answer, he used work as his excuse to ask whoever was asking him what he didn't want to face to leave. She wasn't about to let him do it today.

"I don't care what you have on that desk that is so important, Pa, but quite frankly, I don't care. This is important. This is my future. I don't want to marry Herbert Miller. I don't love him. You've got to put a stop to this."

He reached up and rubbed his fingers into his temples. "What is it that you want me to say, Abby? I don't have time for this."

"I want you to say no and tell him that I'm not ready to marry and that you don't give him your blessing."

"You know I can't say that, young lady."

"For heaven's sakes, why not?"

"Because we've already agreed, and he's already paid off our debts."

"He's done what?" She didn't mean to shout, but she did anyway, and the look on her father's face as the loudness in her tone blared in his ears told her she should have given a second thought before letting her volume raise.

"Don't take that tone with me, young lady."

"I'm sorry, Pa. I didn't mean to. It's just that . . . I don't want to marry Herbert Miller."

"And I don't understand why you don't. He comes from a good family—"

"And he wants to provide me with a good life. I know." She threw her hands up in the air and paced in front of her father's desk. "Mother already told me all those things. But they don't matter. It doesn't matter how good his family is or what he wants to provide for me. I don't want to be like my sisters. You know this. You've always known this."

"Don't tell me you still have all those silly notions of adventure stuck in your head."

"They aren't silly."

"But they are!" He slapped his hand down on his desk. The force was so great that it rattled the oil lamp sitting on the edge, and the flame flickered. Abby flinched, and she stared at her pa, blinking.

Of course, she'd seen her father angry a time or two growing up. She didn't think there was a child alive who didn't see their parents in a fit at least once. It was what adults did.

But while she knew he could get that angry, she didn't expect to see it. At least not today. Not over this.

He fetched an envelope, opened it, and yanked out the money tucked inside. He threw it down on the table. "Do you see this? This is what will save this family. You are what will save this family. Abby, it's time you grow up and stop wasting your time and thoughts on silly things. You're not a child anymore. You're a woman. It's time for you to marry and take care of a husband and children. I know you have never talked about wanting those things, but I thought perhaps the older you became . . ."

"Well, you thought wrong." She folded her arms across her chest.

"Perhaps I did. But that doesn't change the fact that we will make the wedding plans when this young man comes over this afternoon."

"Pa, please, no. Don't make me do this."

He held up his hands. "I'm sorry, Abby, but I've already made my decision, and the deal is done. It's what I had to do to save this house and my family. And it was the best thing I could have done for you." He moved to the office door, opening it before he paused in the frame. "Now, if you'll excuse me, I must see to the rest of my work before this young man arrives."

"Pa?"

"Abby, this conversation is finished."

Tears welled in her eyes, and although she tried to blink them away, she couldn't, and they soon found themselves spilling over and streaming down her cheeks. She shook her head as she watched him leave the office. While she knew there had been a chance he wouldn't listen to her, she hoped he might.

And now that hope was gone, leaving her with only a sense of desperation.

What could she do? She couldn't marry Herbert. She just couldn't. She would rather run away than marry him.

Run away.

That was what she would do.

That was the answer.

If she wanted adventure when no one would give it to her, well then, she would simply take it for herself.

All she needed was to pack some clothes and get her hands on some money.

Money.

She glanced over her shoulder toward the pile of cash Pa had yanked out of the envelope. She didn't know how much was there, but it looked enough. Or she should say it looked like enough to get her where she wanted to go. It was hers after all, wasn't it? If she was the one sold like a farm animal?

She moved over to the desk, staring down at the paper bills.

She didn't have to take it all. She could leave some of it for her parents.

Never mind, she thought. *I'm taking every last dollar.*

TWO

WILLIAM

"*D*o you have room for my horse?"

William's eyes fluttered with the booming voice that filtered into the barn from the stalls and walkway below. He rolled over, and several stalks of hay poked his back through his shirt. He hated sleeping in the hayloft of a barn, but it was safer than sleeping in a stall. Not only could a horse step on him, or worse, lay down on him in a stall, but there was a better chance he would get caught if he was down there instead of up in the hayloft.

And he couldn't get caught.

Not unless he wanted to go to jail.

Which he didn't.

"Yeah. Just take the last stall on the left, Mr. Russell. Are you boarding for the day?" another voice asked.

"I'll be back for him around dawn. That's when we leave to take another trip to Oregon. I gots me a pocket full of money, and I want to have fun spending it."

William's ears perked up with the word money, and he rolled over again, scooting on his stomach toward the edge of the loft so he could look down upon the man. He couldn't glimpse the man's face looking down on the top of his hat, but the man was dressed in all black from his hat to his chaps. He watched as the man led his buckskin horse down the walkway into the stall and untacked it before throwing the saddle on the rack and hooking the bridle on the horn. He fed and watered the animal, then strode back toward the door. The rowels of his spurs clanked and rattled with each of his steps.

William knew he needed to get out of the barn before the stable master found him. He didn't know the price he would have to pay if caught sleeping in the hayloft, but he wasn't about to find out. He rolled up onto his knees, folding his blanket before shoving it in his bag and brushing the last crumbs of the stale loaf of bread he had for dinner, so they scattered in the hay.

Looking over the edge of the loft, he glanced around, and after making sure no one would see him, he scaled down the ladder, jumping off the last rung before he slung his bag over his shoulder and darted out the back door of the barn.

～

*W*illiam hadn't ever been to Independence, Missouri before. He'd only heard about it in his brother's stories. They used to talk about coming here as young boys when they dreamed. It was known as the Queen City of the Trails. The starting point where those seeking to travel out west to the frontier started their journey. He hadn't known what to expect from this strange little city, but such didn't matter. All that did was that somehow, he found his way out of it.

And preferably by wagon on a wagon train headed to Oregon or California.

He wasn't picky about where he would go. He just needed to

get as far away from Missouri as possible and by any means he could.

Even if he had to work for it.

He trotted down the different alleyways between the buildings, staying off the main streets as he veered through town. He rounded the corner onto another street, and as he did, he came face to face with a small café. Scents of eggs, bacon, sausage, and potatoes wafted in the air, and his stomach growled as though to tell him it wanted everything the nose could smell. His mouth watered too, and he closed his eyes, imagining how it all tasted—which he was sure was delicious.

He hadn't eaten anything since finding that loaf of old bread in the garbage outside of the bakery yesterday morning, and while he had planned to go back there to check for more, the thought of stale, butterless bread was no match for the smell of a hot breakfast.

Opening his eyes, he glanced down at the ground. He didn't want more stale bread any more than he wanted to dig out his own eyes, but of course, there was one big problem. How to get it? Getting the bread was easy, but with empty pockets and not a nickel to his name, the hot breakfast was nothing short of impossible.

He heaved a deep sigh and hunched his shoulders as he kicked at a rock and watched it roll several inches. Admitting defeat was never easy, and this morning with a grumbling stomach was no exception.

Still, facts were facts. He didn't have the money, so bread it was.

He continued down the street, barely looking up as he passed the café. He didn't want to see the food any more than he wanted to smell it, but as he passed, he glanced out of the corner of his eye. A young couple was sitting at a table outside, chatting to one another. Distracted with their conversation, they didn't even look at William as he passed. Hesitation spurred through him, and he slowed down, watching as the man scooted his chair toward the woman, and they huddled their faces close to one another.

"And so, I told him, Mr. Dexter, I just can't marry your daughter because I'm in love with someone else," the man said.

"Oh, and just who might that be?" the woman asked.

The man scooted his chair even closer and grabbed her hands. "Why, you, my darling." While the woman ducked her chin, her face turned a bright shade of red, and she removed her handkerchief from her handbag, brushing her other hand along her chest. William wanted to retch at the sight of their love and affection for one another, but with an empty stomach, nothing would have come up. Not to mention, he would have drawn unwanted attention from what he was about to do.

He just needed to wait for the perfect moment . . .

Just as he had hoped, the man, so overcome with love, shoved his plate aside and out of his way. William lunged over the small fence separating the dining area from the sidewalk and grabbed the plate. The woman screamed, but as the man spun in his chair, William took off down the street with the plate tucked tight into his body so none of the food would spill.

～

*W*illiam continued down the street and around another building, hiding behind several wooden crates stacked against the brick wall. He pressed his back against the bricks and glanced down both directions of the alleyway before sliding down to the ground and tucking his legs up until he was blocked from sight.

His lungs heaved, and he closed his eyes. "Lord. Please forgive me for stealing this food. I know it's wrong, and I have sinned. I hate to eat it, but . . . I'm starving. I pray for my forgiveness. In Jesus' name. Amen."

Although the first bite tasted like a little bit of heaven, the guilt gave it an unpleasant aftertaste. It was one he didn't like, but he also knew that he didn't know when he would see food again without stealing. He wanted to curse himself just as much as he wanted to curse his brother for putting him into this mess. And yet, he also knew that doing either of those wouldn't make the situation better.

Nothing would make it better.

Well, clearing his name would.

But knowing the solution and putting it into play were two different things. Pinkertons weren't about hearing reason. They just saw the words as excuses. The guilty are always trying to get out of punishment for their crimes, they would say, and no matter what he told them, they would only say it to him.

They wouldn't believe him.

Nor would they even give him the chance to explain.

He shoveled the last few bites of eggs into his mouth, both wanting to chew them slowly to savor them and also gobble them down so he could flee before anyone caught him. Once he had licked it clean, he tossed the plate aside, and another hint of guilt prickled in his chest as the bone white china smacked against the dirt with a thud sound. He wanted to return the plate to the café, and yet he knew that it would be foolish to do so.

Perhaps I can leave it outside the door tonight after dark, he thought. Do at least one good thing today, even if it's not much of one.

It would be the right thing to do.

He could almost hear his mama talking to him from Heaven above, telling him what he needed to do. Or course, that was nothing new. He listened to her daily, always on his case about one thing or another he did. Lord, she would roll over in her grave if she saw him now. He was glad she passed on so she wouldn't have to see the utter failure he'd become. As much as he hated to think that, he did, and it was just another thing to hate his brother for.

He heaved a deep sigh and slipped his hand into his pants pocket, pulling out a folded piece of paper. It was yellower than it had been months ago, and the edges were tearing from all the time spent in his pocket, and all the times he pulled it out, looked at it, and stuck it back in. It wasn't that looking at it gave him hope or comfort. It was just the opposite, actually. The paper only brought him fear, pain, and anger, and although he wanted to throw it away every second of every day, he also wanted to keep it. He didn't know why.

Perhaps it was the reminder he needed.

Or perhaps he was nothing but an utter fool.

He didn't know which.

But as he opened it and looked down upon the words 'WANTED' and a drawn picture of his face with his name below written in black ink, all the feelings came flooding back.

He was a wanted man.

And it was all his brother's fault.

ORDER OR READ FOR FREE WITH KINDLE UNLIMITED

To my sister
Michelle Renee Horning

April 3, 1973 - January 8, 2022
You will be forever missed. I don't know how I'm going to do this thing
called life without you.

LONDON JAMES IS A PEN NAME FOR ANGELA CHRISTINA ARCHER. SHE LIVES ON A RANCH WITH HER HUSBAND, TWO DAUGHTERS, AND MANY FARM ANIMALS. SHE WAS BORN AND RAISED IN NEVADA AND GREW UP RIDING AND SHOWING HORSES. WHILE SHE DOESN'T SHOW ANYMORE, SHE STILL LOVES TO TRAIL RIDE.

FROM A YOUNG AGE, SHE ALWAYS WANTED TO WRITE A NOVEL. HOWEVER, EVERY TIME THE DESIRE FLICKERED, SHE SHOVED THE THOUGHT FROM MY MIND UNTIL ONE MORNING IN 2009, SHE AWOKE WITH THE DETERMINATION TO FOLLOW HER DREAM.

WWW.AUTHORLONDONJAMES.COM

JOIN MY MAILING LIST FOR NEWS ON RELEASES, DISCOUNTED SALES, AND EXCLUSIVE MEMBER-ONLY BENEFITS!

Copyright © 2022

Cover Design by Angela Archer, Long Valley Designs

This book is a work of fiction. The names, characters, places, and incidents are the products of the author's imagination or are used fictitiously.

Any resemblance to actual events, business establishments, locales, or persons, living or dead, is entirely coincidental.

All rights reserved.

No part of this publication may be reproduced, stored in retrieval system, or transmitted in any form or by any means (electronic, mechanical, photocopying, recording, or otherwise) without prior written permission of both the copyright owner and the publisher. The only exception is brief quotations in printed reviews.

The scanning, uploading, and distribution of this book via the Internet or via any other means without the permission of the publisher is illegal and punishable by law.

Please purchase only authorized electronic editions and do not participate in or encourage electronic piracy of copyrighted materials.

Your support of the author's rights is appreciated.

Published in the United States of America by:

Long Valley Press
Newcastle, Oklahoma
WWW.LONGVALLEYPRESS.COM

Scriptures taken from the Holy Bible, New International Version®, NIV®. Copyright © 1973, 1978, 1984, 2011 by Biblica, Inc.™ Used by permission of Zondervan. All rights reserved worldwide. WWW.ZONDERVAN.COM The "NIV" and "New International Version" are trademarks registered in the United States Patent and Trademark Office by Biblica, Inc.™

Made in the USA
Middletown, DE
14 April 2023

28867343R00094